Sky Hunter

Carmen Colorado

Clara Ann Simons

Sky Hunter

Carmen Colorado

Clara Ann Simons

Index

Chapter 1

Gabriela

In the air, I'm free. On solid ground, each step is a mask I must maintain.

The F-35 roars beneath my hands as I execute the final approach to Zelenova Base. Behind me, the rest of the squadron lines up in perfect formation, one we've held since takeoff from the carrier. Ghost, Reaper, Bulldog, and Shadow follow my lead like we're a single mind split between five bodies.

"Night Hawk, you're cleared to land on runway one," the controller's voice crackles through the radio.

I touch down with practiced grace, the result of thousands of flight hours. The runway stretches before us like a long gray scar cutting through a snowy landscape that looks spectacular from above.

On the ground, technicians rush toward us as soon as we kill the engines. They're efficient and professional , but can't help staring at our aircraft like kids eyeing Christmas presents. I guess it's not every day a small base like this receives an F-35 squadron.

"Welcome to Zelenova, Major Díaz," a young lieutenant greets me as I descend the ladder. "It's an honor to have the Night Specters with us."

I smile hearing our nickname. Officially, we're the 401st Fighter Squadron of the Air Force, though everyone knows us by our callsign.

"My new home for the next few months," I mutter under my breath.

Or at least until the situation in the Middle East gets complicated enough that they need us there. It's no coincidence they've stationed the Air Force's best unit at a base so close to the conflict zone.

"Night Hawk!" Ghost shouts, approaching with long strides. "Did you see that snowy landscape from the sky? I think I'm gonna like this place."

Rick "Ghost" Miller has been my wingman for the past three years. He's the best combat pilot I know, though I'd never admit that to his face. His black hair gleams under the winter sun as he surveys the base, seeming not to miss a single detail.

The other pilots join us, joking about the cold as we head toward the main building. We're a diverse group, united by the sky and adrenaline. In the air, we communicate without words. On ground, jokes and combat callsigns are our trademark.

I have to admit, the base is impressive—one of the best I've been assigned to. Concrete and steel buildings rise against the gray sky, designed to withstand an attack if necessary. Underground hangars capable of protecting our aircraft in case of bombing—a masterpiece of military engineering. Everything is designed so we can take off within fifteen minutes if the situation demands it.

"Your house, Major," the lieutenant announces, stopping in front of a row of attached houses. "If you need anything, just let me know."

All senior officers have individual housing with small gardens. The interior is functional but cozy. Standard army furniture, though good quality. A well-equipped kitchen, though I doubt I'll use it much. A bedroom with mountain views. Could be worse. Much worse.

"Briefings are at 0700 every morning," the lieutenant continues. "Colonel Anderson wants to see you in his office at 1600 hours."

I nod while looking out the window. From here, I can clearly see the village of Zelenova with its red roofs covered in snow—the last snowfall of the year—and the church tower rising above the houses as if pointing to the sky. It's a picturesque place, almost like a Christmas post-card.

"The village is only a twenty-minute walk," the lieutenant adds, noticing my gaze. "There are some pretty good restaurants if you ever prefer not to eat on base."

I wonder what it's like to live here, in this small corner of Europe where time seems to have stopped. It's very different from the other bases I've been stationed at. Quieter. More… civilian.

Ghost appears at the door without knocking, as usual.

"They've got a state-of-the-art simulator for us. We should try it this afternoon."

I smile. Some things never change. No matter where we are or what country we're assigned to, Ghost always finds a way to turn any situation into a competition.

"After the meeting with Anderson," I respond. "I'm going to kick your ass."

"We'll see, Night Hawk. We'll see," he murmurs as he leaves.

I watch him walk away down the snowy path. He whistles an old tune that resonates in the cold afternoon air. Up here, so close to the mountains, even sounds seem different.

I take a deep breath, the cold air filling my lungs. A new posting. A new mission. And the constant feeling that something is about to change.

***

Centuries of history reflect in every building of Zelenova as I walk its streets. There's tranquility in the air, almost happiness. I smile, observing the friendliness of the locals. They greet me as I pass. Beyond, a group of children plays soccer in a park despite the cold. This place has a special charm. Its cobblestone streets, historic houses and monuments, the good atmosphere that permeates everything.

"I wish I could be stationed here for a good long while," I murmur to myself as I continue walking.

Minutes later, I stop in front of a storefront that catches my attention. "Emma's Literary Café."

"Coffee and books in one place. Exactly what I need," I sigh.

A small bell tinkles as I push open the heavy door. Immediately, a wave of aromas hits me. They strike with such force I can almost taste them: freshly brewed coffee, cinnamon, the unique smell of paper books. Sunlight filters lazily through the curtains, drawing strange patterns on a row of dark wooden tables. Some villagers converse quietly while holding their coffee cups. Others have lost themselves between the pages of books. This place breathes peace.

My eyes linger on an enormous bookshelf occupying an entire wall. Books pile from floor to ceiling, a perfect mix of classics and latest releases. Many of them in English.

"Welcome to the Literary Café," a soft voice catches my attention. "Can I help you?"

I turn to respond, and the world stops. The most beautiful green eyes I've ever seen observe me with curiosity. The gorgeous woman before me, with that elegance and smile, stirs something inside me. So much that I even get nervous, something that rarely happens.

"H-hello," I feel heat in my cheeks, and I'm sure I'm blushing slightly. "Actually, yes, I'm new in town, just assigned to the base, and when I saw your storefront, I felt really curious."

"Then I must welcome you and offer you coffee," she proposes with an elegant gesture of her hand, inviting me to follow her. "Sorry, is it okay if I use the informal 'you'?"

I simply nod.

"Here you have everything you need to have a good time and find tranquility. As you can see, we serve all kinds of coffee, pastries and sweets, and you can enjoy them with a good book."

I look around at the same time she does, absorbing each of her words and the feeling they carry.

"It really is a wonderful place. Coffee and reading. The two passions of my life," I joke, and we both laugh. "Especially when work allows."

"May I ask what you do? I mean, you're American, and you mentioned being stationed at the base. Let me guess! You observe everything with such attention. Do you work in aircraft maintenance? Wait! First, what kind of coffee do you prefer?"

"An Americano, please," I respond with a smile.

"Coming right up! So, did I guess right?"

"Not quite. I'm a fighter pilot. I'll be stationed at the base for a while."

"I lived on that base too, a long time ago, and many others actually," she confesses, and my eyes widen in surprise, provoking another of her laughs that make my heart race. "My mother was in the Air Force."

"And you came back to this town? You liked it that much?"

"I fell in love with Zelenova, with its people, with everything. It's a magical place, you'll see. A little over two years ago, I divorced my husband and came back. I set up the café, and I've been here since."

"Wow! That's a really interesting story."

The conversation flows naturally while she shows me around. I lose myself in her gestures, in the way her hand briefly caresses my arm, in how her green eyes seem to sparkle every time she mentions something she's passionate about. Sometimes, I could swear she's flirting with me, but then I remember she mentioned an ex-husband and my hopes deflate like a punctured balloon.

She apologizes when some customers call her, a moment I use to observe her and rediscover that she's absolutely charming. She always wears a smile and seems to enjoy helping whenever someone has a question.

In the end, I choose a book about local history that, for some strange reason, catches my attention. I return to the counter and wait for the two gentlemen in front of me to finish their orders.

"I'll take this," I announce, placing it in front of her. "You've sold this town to me so well that I want to know more."

She smiles, and everything inside me stirs again.

"You'll love it. Although if you really want to get to know it, I'd advise spending a lot of time here. Whenever you can, of course."

"I'll come often, I promise."

"Well, if you ever need my help, you know where to find me."

She hands me the book, neatly stored in a bag. I pay, and before leaving, I decide to introduce myself.

"I'm Gabriela, by the way."

"Emma," she responds, extending her hand. The contact sends an electric current through my entire arm. "It's been a pleasure meeting you. Come back anytime."

And as I step out onto the street, I know I'll return. Something tells me I'll come back as often as I can, if only to see that smile and those beautiful green eyes.

Chapter 2

Emma

Mornings at the Literary Café border on magical. Regular customers settle into their usual spots while light filters lazily through the windows. The aroma of freshly brewed coffee mingles with the scent of plants I've strategically placed to breathe life into the space. Spring hovers just around the corner; I feel it in the air, in the light that grows brighter each day.

I watch curious passersby enter, drawn in by the display window or the smell of homemade pastries. Most just take a quick glance before leaving. Still, each time the doorbell chimes, my heart skips a beat. I look up hoping to see Gabriela. She said she'd return, but several days have passed since her visit, and I surprise myself by missing her despite barely knowing her.

She's a woman who attracts me somehow. I must admit that during my marriage, I felt curiosity and fascination for some women, but I've never had a relationship with them. Not physical or any other kind.

"You really like this girl, don't you?" Lucille, my assistant and best friend, inquires, approaching me with tiny steps. "You met her for a few minutes and you can't stop talking about her."

"She has something special," I admit, wiping a nonexistent stain from the counter. "I can't even describe it. But no," I deny, not wanting to overthink it, "I really think it's because I'm feeling lonely, and it's been too long without sex. One more month and I might go crazy."

"Well, all the more reason, Emma! Life's too short to pass up something sweet. Go for it. You're both adults and can do whatever you want."

"Come on, don't be silly. I don't think she even noticed me. And besides, I haven't seen her again. She probably has a lot of work at the base."

Feeling nervous, I quickly change the subject, telling her my plan to set up a booth at the Zora Fest. The festival is a town tradition and a perfect opportunity to promote the café. Still, the pilot refuses to leave my thoughts, no matter how hard I try.

"The Literary Café needs to be there and become better known, you never know when or where new customers might appear," I point out, convinced of this.

"Knowing how hardworking and detail-oriented you are, it'll be the most beautiful and well-crafted booth of all. Plus, everyone knows you around here, I'm sure you'll make lots of sales."

"You think so?"

"I guarantee it, friend," she nods confidently. "In fact, if you want, I can lend you a hand. I love decorating, and I didn't do so badly at previous festivals."

"You don't mind?" I ask, flustered. "I'm sure you're busy."

"Don't worry. Setting up the booth for the festival will be a piece of cake. Besides," that mischievous expression so characteristic of her suddenly appears, "I want to see you talking with that woman, Gabriela."

"You don't even know if she'll come!" I add defensively, blushing.

"Something tells me she will," she whispers, pointing to her nose.

I roll my eyes while she laughs. The afternoon progresses with customers coming and going, books finding new readers, and coffee cups emptying. I look around my little bookstore and can't help but smile. When I opened it, I never thought it would become a sanctuary for so many people, a space where people could rediscover the pleasure of reading. Some customers have told me they've started reading again thanks to my recommendations. Just for that, I feel satisfied.

***

The afternoon descends lazily over Zelenova as I push my cart through the supermarket aisles. I like to shop before reopening the café after lunch break, wanting to ensure we never run out of anything when customers start filling the tables.

I review my list and look at the shelf packed with coffee boxes. Lately, I've been thinking about making some changes, perhaps adding a more intense variety. I stand on tiptoe and stretch to reach a box on the top shelf, and as I grab it, the one next to it wobbles. I instinctively close my eyes, expecting impact, though it never comes. I wait for the crash on the floor, but that doesn't happen either.

"Are you okay? It almost hit you on the head; lucky I reached it in time."

That voice. My heart skips several beats as I turn and find Gabriela holding the box with a smile that illuminates the entire supermarket.

"Yes, yes, I'm fine," I respond, composing myself and trying to hide my nervousness. "And thank you. I think you saved me from a real mess. These boxes wouldn't survive a fall, and everything would have spilled everywhere."

Her eyes linger on the boxes in my hands while she puts the one she caught back in its place.

"I was planning to stop by the café now; I've had some exhausting days and needed a little quiet time."

"I'm heading there as soon as I finish shopping. If you want, you can come with me," I suggest, perhaps with too much enthusiasm.

"I'd love to," she responds with a smile that makes my knees weak.

We walk the aisles together, laughing when our carts collide as we search for what we need.

"I'm surprised to see you shopping here," I comment. "Most officers stay at the base's hypermarket."

"I like to escape and just be Gabriela for a while," she confesses, shrugging naturally. "Not that shopping is my favorite hobby," she adds, playfully, making me laugh. "But you know what I mean."

As we leave the store, we continue our conversation until we reach the café. She's different from other combat pilots I've met. There's no arrogance in her way of speaking, just an honesty that makes me want to know her better. She likes to go out and be herself, meet people, and above all, help when needed. She doesn't look down on us like the rest usually do, feeling superior for being the elite within the air force. Plus, she's very open-minded in every way, and I like that.

I tell her that in a few days there's a traditional festival where she can discover all kinds of things about Zelenova. From its food to typical decorations. Whatever she's interested in, she'll be able to see it.

"I love it! And you say it's this weekend?"

"Yes, that's right."

"Will you be there?" she asks with a look that melts me.

"Yes, I'll have my own booth. Books and coffee," I respond, trying to maintain a casual tone.

"Well! Then I won't miss it," she adds, with a wink that leaves me breathless.

Is she flirting with me? As we enter the café and I prepare everything for opening, I can't stop feeling her gaze. She accompanies me and helps with whatever I need, even picking up a couple of boxes of books I was planning to open and arrange.

"Where do you want me to put these?" she asks, showing no strain at all.

"Here, on this table," I point. "Are you sure they're not too heavy?"

"I train daily," she responds naturally. "My job requires it."

"That's obvious," I blurt out almost without thinking as I look at her. Her smile appears when our eyes meet. She's made me blush. I clear my throat before continuing to speak. "I mean, you're very strong; it's clear you take care of yourself."

"Yes, quite a bit."

"Maybe I should follow your example a little, it's been too long since I exercised," I admit, rolling my eyes.

"It's hard to get back into it, but once you establish a routine, everything gets easier. If you want, I can help you. I could give you some tips and even train together," she offers.

Her offer catches me by surprise. The idea of spending more time with her is tempting, dangerously tempting.

"Would you really do that?"

"Of course."

"I'll try to rearrange my schedule then and let you know. With the festival now, I don't think I'll have much free time."

"Don't worry, I understand. No pressure, whenever you can."

The fact that she understands my work and my timing without even knowing me captivates me. I don't think anyone has ever treated me with such respect and care as she does. Each moment I spend by her side makes me realize she's different, and that both appeals to and frightens me. Memories from the past hit me, painfully reminding me that I could get hurt again, and I don't want that. Even more so, considering this would be my first relationship with a woman.

Too many doubts assault me, and I'm not even sure she likes me. Maybe she's just being nice. I don't know, I think the best thing is to forget about this and move on with my life. Besides, her presence is temporary;

when the work is done, she'll leave again, they'll station her far from here, and I don't want to suffer. Better to turn the page and not overthink it.

Chapter 3

Gabriela

What are you doing here? A voice repeats in my head as I arrive at the Zora Fest. I know I should be resting instead of spending the night at a festival. Yet, this inner critic falls silent as I move through the grounds, discovering the wonders of this town—its cuisine, decorations, pottery… I think there's nothing that doesn't catch my eye. Still, I admit I didn't come to see all this, though I love it. I traded my sleep hours simply to see her.

I keep walking until I reach her booth, ignoring everything around me. The flower bouquets, the sweets, and the coffee aroma make it stand out from the others. That and the long line in front of it. People crowd around while she works practically alone, so I decide to wait at a distance, not wanting to add to her stress.

"It won't take long for her to get rid of each and every one of them," a woman positions herself beside me as I observe Emma's booth from afar.

I can't help studying her, analyzing her like I would any new element in a mission: medium height, brown hair gathered in a casual braid, and intense blue eyes that examine me with a mixture of curiosity and possibly amusement. There's an air of familiarity in her relaxed posture, in the way her eyes keep shifting between Emma and me. I'd say she's a friend or relative. In fact, I'm completely sure by the way she's looking at me.

"I'm Lucille, her best friend," she clarifies.

"Nice to meet you. I'm—"

"Gabriela, I know," she interjects before I can continue, "she's told me about you."

I raise my eyebrows, surprised by the confession, wondering what Emma might have said.

"I hope you don't mind that she mentioned you," Lucille continues, lowering her voice slightly as if sharing a secret. "Actually, don't even mention it to her, please. She'd kill me."

I can't help laughing at that last phrase.

"Don't worry," I continue, still smiling. "My lips are sealed."

As minutes pass, the last customer leaves the booth, and I see my opportunity to approach. Lucille, who had remained beside me in comfortable silence, leaves without saying goodbye, as suddenly as she appeared. I'm fascinated by how direct and honest she was during our brief encounter. I'm starting to like her.

I approach the booth, watching Emma collapse into a small folding chair, clearly exhausted. But when she sees me, she stands up again.

"No, no, please sit," I say before she can speak. "I've seen how hard you've been working, and you deserve to rest a bit."

Her look is a mixture of surprise and gratitude. She hesitates for the briefest moment but finally heeds my words, sitting back down with a sigh of relief. I allow myself to pass to her side, staying a couple of feet away.

"Are you okay?" I ask, noticing the fatigue in her eyes.

"Yes, it's just that this year the market has exceeded all my expectations. I haven't stopped in the last few hours," she admits, running a hand through her hair.

"Have you eaten anything?"

"Well, if a bite of a croissant and half a coffee count as eating…"

"That's not good," I murmur, shaking my head. I look around, spotting a food stand a few yards ahead. "Don't move from here, I'll be right back."

A few minutes later, I walk toward her with a couple of bags filled with tortillas stuffed with cheese, avocado, chicken, and lettuce. Plus a bottle of water and a soda.

"It's the most nutritious thing I could find," I apologize, hurried.

"You didn't have to do this, Gabriela," she says with a beautiful smile while inspecting the contents of the bags. She lightly bites her lower lip as she catches the scent of the freshly made tortillas.

"Come on, eat something."

She must be starving to not even argue with me. To my surprise, she fully opens the bags and places them so we both can easily access the contents. I didn't expect her to share with me, but I haven't had dinner, and my stomach appreciates it with a slight growl that makes me blush.

"This is delicious. Thank you," she murmurs after the first bite.

"Don't mention it. In fact, I'm pretty sure the man is angry with me," I state, about to laugh.

"Why? What did you say to him?"

"He was trying to give me cold, stale food, and I had to call him out to prevent that from happening."

I swear that when we turn to observe him from afar, the man looks at us grumpily. A gesture that makes us burst into laughter.

"That's Harold," she explains, covering her mouth between laughs. "He cooks wonderfully, but every so often he tries to pull a fast one and slip some cold plates to strangers. The fact that you stood up to him will have him sulking until tomorrow."

"That's his problem. I wasn't going to let him do it," I assure her.

Minutes pass between laughter and conversations. The food disappears quickly, and Emma keeps thanking me for the gesture, though really I should be the grateful one. It's been a long time since I felt so comfortable with someone.

"How come you're not resting at the base?" she suddenly asks. "I'm sure you'll have to work again in a few hours."

"I wanted to discover the Zora Fest. It's my first time seeing one of these festivals in this part of Europe, especially during the early morning hours. It's incredible that, despite the time, the whole town is gathered here."

"It really is wonderful," she nods and gives me a slightly melancholic look that makes her even more beautiful if possible. "It's a tradition that brings us together every year and makes living together magnificent. Although, the most beautiful part is the Dawn Dance."

"The Dawn Dance?" I inquire, raising my eyebrows.

"People gather in the square just before dawn, with lanterns. We dance while the first rays of sunlight shine on us," she explains with contagious enthusiasm. "It's symbolic. It represents new beginnings and the unity of the town."

"Wow, that must be beautiful."

"It is," she sighs.

Hours pass before our eyes as we engage in a conversation that allows us to get to know each other better. We discover common interests: reading, certain types of food, and even some singers we both admire. It's amazing how, without trying, life leads you to people who you know will mark you deeply in your heart.

Some time later, the quick steps of people catch my attention. Emma checks the time and stands up.

"Come on! Come with me." She takes my hand and pulls me in the same direction as everyone else.

"Where are we going in such a hurry?"

"Don't you want to witness the Dawn Dance?" With a simple look, my answer is yes, a gesture that makes her smile and squeeze my fingers even more.

When we reach the square, the entire town seems to have gathered in perfect harmony. They remain silent before the start of a song. Each note builds the peace and tranquility that the place transmits. The union of all the people gathered there. I realize that people start dancing to the melody. So I look at her and with a simple movement, I ask her to dance and join the others. I think she hesitates for a brief moment, but she takes my hands and moves closer until our bodies brush against each other.

I'm sure everyone is looking at the beautiful sunrise unfolding to our right. However, all I can look at are those wonderful green eyes in front of me. I watch, fascinated, how her pupils change with the growing light, how each nascent sunbeam seems to enhance her beauty to impossible limits.

We move together, dancing close. Without stopping our gaze, forgetting everything around us. Every time Emma looks at me, I melt, and my desire to kiss her rises considerably to the point that it burns inside me. I want to do it, I need it like air to breathe. But something in my head makes me stop just before joining my lips to hers. I'm not sure that kissing her in front of everyone, especially without knowing if she likes me or even if she likes women, is a good idea. The signals she sends are confusing, and for now, I decide not to continue.

I rest my forehead against hers, avoiding what I want so badly, and hearing a sigh from her that makes me think again about the mistake I've made by not doing it. Too many doubts and uncertainties pass through my mind.

Chapter 4

Gabriela

Two days have passed since what happened in the town square. Forty-eight hours where my head thinks only of Emma. Of that almost-kiss I still desire with every fiber of my being. I'm too confused. She's become an obsession that accompanies me during maneuvers. She's with me in officer meetings, even in brief moments of rest.

Dawn at a military base differs vastly from civilian life. Our days begin early. After years of rigorous training, my body has adapted and responds mechanically.

The moment my bare feet touch the floor, I feel the cold, though it helps clear my head. In the bathroom mirror, I observe a woman with sleep in her eyes, with tousled hair. The pillow's imprint still marks my cheek. This is the real Gabriela, the woman they don't see at the base. Someone very different from Night Hawk, the cold combat pilot.

I shake my head. I try to push these thoughts from my mind and step into the shower. Five minutes of cold water. A ritual that awakens every atom in my body. The icy water falls forcefully on my back and washes away the last traces of sleep. As I dry myself with the towel, the base wakes up. In the distance, I hear a dog barking, hurried footsteps, orders coming from the barracks. The military machinery kicks into operation with a precision rehearsed daily.

I adjust my uniform and pull my hair into a bun. I don't like makeup. Just a touch of concealer. Sobriety is one of my identifying marks.

Ghost is already there when I enter the officers' cafeteria. The rest of the team will arrive shortly. Nobody's late. Ever. It's a habit we've had for years. We have breakfast together every day instead of each eating in our own quarters.

The rest of the military personnel look at us with a mixture of respect and wariness. I understand—we just arrived and we're an elite unit. They know well that if we're here, it's because things will get ugly any moment.

After breakfast, I explain to my squadron the flight maneuvers for this morning. The pilots form a semicircle around me. Nobody questions orders.

Nobody detects that, beneath the uniform, my heart beats faster each time I think about green eyes I'm starting to fall in love with.

Soon we're in the air. Up here, everything boils down to an instrument panel and the immensity of the sky. Here everything is much simpler yet more intense. For a few hours, I'll forget the dilemma tearing me apart inside.

I don't hide who I am. Nor am I ashamed of my sexual orientation. I fought that battle years ago, and it was much easier than I thought back then. Still, combat pilots sit at the top of the pyramid. I've learned to maintain a low profile in my personal life. I prefer not having to find out if everyone in my squadron agrees with this part of me. I've heard enough casual comments, too many tasteless jokes. I know official regulations protect me, but reality is much more complex. Easier to maintain a division: Night Hawk, the combat pilot, on base. Gabriela, the woman, off it.

On the other hand, I'm not even sure if Emma feels the same way I do or understands what's happening between us. The fact that she was married to a man means nothing, I know. I know many women who discovered their sexuality after marrying men. And yet, those prolonged glances, those seemingly innocent touches… Maybe it's just my imagination. I prefer not to risk it and get slapped— I've taken enough hits in my life.

"Everything okay, Night Hawk?" Ghost asks while dropping some papers on my desk after the flight session. "You've been… absent for hours."

I simply nod and smile.

The afternoon drags on endlessly at the base. Free time becomes unbearable. After turning it over in my mind countless times, I decide to return to the Literary Café. I haven't finished reading the book I took, but I'm dying to see her. I'm starting to accept that we'll be nothing more than friends, and I think that's for the best. While I drive, a song about impossible love plays. What irony.

That peculiar aroma envelops me the moment I step into the establishment. I observe a couple of groups animatedly discussing the book they hold. A curious browser examines the shelves while running fingertips along the spines, as if searching for hidden treasure.

And then I see her.

She wobbles while carrying boxes that are too heavy. I run to help her before she can hurt herself.

"You shouldn't carry this alone, it's too heavy," I indicate while placing it where she directs me.

"I don't have much choice, Gabriela… And, thank you," she sighs as she tucks a strand of hair behind her ear, making my pulse quicken.

"My pleasure," I admit with a smile, though I sense she's a little sad. "Are you okay?"

"Yes, it's just that I have a lot of work. The festival brought me new customers, and I've had to receive many orders," she explains, maintaining a casual tone.

"That's great news, isn't it?"

"It is…" she sighs, looking away when our eyes meet. "Everything good at the base? It's been two days since I've seen you."

Has she been counting the hours too? Has she been prey to this strange anxiety?

"Lots of work too; it's a somewhat complicated time, but yes, everything's fine."

"What happened to your forehead?" she questions with concern, pointing at it with her index finger.

"War wounds, you know," I joke, though it doesn't seem to amuse her. "I bumped myself while training. Lost my balance and smacked into the wall. These things happen," I add, shrugging.

"Are you sure you're okay?"

To my surprise, she comes closer and gently touches the wound, making sure everything's all right. Her proximity roots me to the spot. Her nose is barely an inch from mine. I can feel her breath on my skin. Even count the tiny freckles on her cheekbones. I stifle a sigh in my throat.

"Yes... I'm fine," I whisper. She looks at me, aware of how close we are.

Her eyes shine now. The sadness has vanished.

She pulls away when a customer approaches, attending to them immediately. Just in time. Five more seconds, and I would have lunged for her lips.

With my heart racing, I decide to look at the shelves again in search of new reading material. I barely pay attention, too conscious of Emma's presence across the room. I sit at one of the most secluded tables, next to a window. From here, I can observe her without seeming like a stalker. God, I'm lost. Especially every time she looks at me and smiles.

Five minutes later she approaches with a coffee in hand and sets it on the table. She's remembered how I like it. She gives it to me with a wink, and I feel my entire being burning inside. Is all this real, or am I starting to imagine things? I try to immerse myself in the books in front of me. It's just a vain attempt to silence the voices screaming at me to get up, take her to the most secluded place, and devour her with kisses.

"Are they interesting?" her voice, sometime later, pulls me back from the world of letters I haven't even explored.

"Yes, quite," this answer contains as much truth as lie. I'm sure the books are very good, but I haven't been able to read a single word.

"May I join you?" she asks almost timidly, pointing to the empty chair beside me.

I nod, as nervous as a teenager on a first date. Unintentionally, I briefly glance at her neckline, and my heart skips several beats. This is going from bad to worse, so I decide to play my card to give her a taste of her own medicine.

"I met Lucille a few days ago."

Her cheeks flush a beautiful crimson, making me smile.

"Wh…when?"

"Shortly before going to your booth at the festival. She'll kill me for telling you, but she mentioned you'd talked to her about me."

"What?!" I can't help laughing when she curses under her breath. "I didn't want to... I'm sorry."

"It's okay, Emma. I'm new, we're getting to know each other. I think it's normal to talk about me to your friend."

"How embarrassing," she sighs, bringing a hand to her forehead and shaking her head.

"No! Don't be embarrassed," I reach for one of her hands and squeeze it gently. "I would have done the same thing."

"Have you talked about me to your friends at the base?"

I look down and sigh.

"It's complicated. At the base, I'm Night Hawk, the major everyone must obey. A strong, decisive, direct woman. I've earned their respect above all else. I command a combat squadron. It's not easy for a woman to achieve that," she nods, I know she understands. "But they don't know Gabriela. Only one of my colleagues, Ghost – Rick," I clarify, "knows me a little better. He's the closest thing I have to a real friend. Even so, he doesn't know everything about me."

"It must be very difficult not having someone to… unburden yourself with."

"It is," I murmur, looking away again and realizing that, deep down, I feel very alone. Her thumb caressing my knuckles makes me look at her again.

"I'm here, Gabriela. I know we barely know each other, but the little I know about you, what you tell me, our conversations… I like all that. I love being able to chat about everything and nothing with you. Count on me for whatever you need."

"Do you really mean that?"

"Of course," she responds without hesitation. "You already know where to find me and…"

She takes out the small notebook she carries in her pocket and writes something before tearing off the page and passing it to me.

"That's my personal number. If you ever can't come, because of work or any other reason, you can send me a message or call me."

"You're an incredible person, you know that?" I say directly, making her blush again.

"You don't really mean that."

"I've never been more serious," I affirm. "I still don't understand how that man, your ex-husband, let you slip away."

Her expression changes slightly when I mention him. Her posture tenses.

"Actually, I was the one who escaped from him," the tone of her voice puts my entire body on alert.

"What do you mean?" I inquire, frowning.

"He was and is a very toxic and manipulative man. At first, I couldn't see the signs. With time, everything became clear. He almost separated me from my best friend, from my people, from this town."

"Fortunately, you got out of there."

"Yes..."

"If he ever decides to come back and do something to you, call me. I won't let him hurt you."

She looks at me, smiles gratefully, and nods without releasing my hand.

For the next few minutes, we engage in lighter conversation: books we've read, movies we like, childhood memories. The tension gradually disappears and ends with an invitation for me to attend a gathering of friends. She insists so much that I'm incapable of denying those green eyes anything. This woman is my absolute undoing.

Chapter 5

Emma

The morning unfolds with its familiar rhythm at the Literary Café. Customers come and go, never leaving without a coffee or a book purchase. Since the festival, the increase in clientele has become noticeable, and that fills me with pride. All those months of sacrifice, doubts, and sleepless nights are finally bearing fruit.

Midmorning, a chill crawls up my spine like a bad omen. I hear the bell above the door tinkle and, for some reason I can't explain, I know something isn't right. I turn, seeking the person to assist them. However, the smile I usually greet people with vanishes the moment I see him.

"What do you think you're doing here?" I question without getting too close.

"Well, I'm glad to see you too," he throws back in that cocky tone he uses when he thinks he's in control. He slips his hands into his pockets and treats me to his typical studied pose of the carefree gentleman.

"What do you want, Daniel?"

My ex-husband never appears without a reason, and his presence never brings anything good.

"Just stopping by to see how everything's going for you," he responds, looking at the place with disgust. It's clear he doesn't like that I have customers.

"Well, as you can see, perfectly," I respond in a dry tone.

"Someone's helping you, right? Admit it. You can't handle all this by yourself."

"You wish," I whisper, holding his gaze, something I wasn't brave enough to do at one time.

"You've always been useless," he spits each word with a bitterness that makes me shudder. "I'm sure you're up to your eyeballs in debt, and your precious little friend Lucille is paying for all this."

"Don't bring my friend into this. And get out of here once and for all. I told you I never wanted to see you again. Do it or..."

"Or what?" he cuts me off, slowly approaching to intimidate me. With each step, he manages to make me instinctively back away, the result of years of

44

psychological and sometimes physical abuse that I haven't completely overcome.

"Leave, Daniel, please," I plead, feeling my eyes fill with tears.

His laugh is a dry sound, full of hate. A diabolical laugh that floods my ears before he disappears through the door. He wanted to scare me, and he succeeded. He made it clear that just by appearing, he can still make me tremble. I take refuge behind the counter, pretending to arrange coffee cups while trying to regain control. A couple of customers observe me discreetly, probably wondering what happened, but no one dares comment.

During the next few hours, I consider canceling the gathering with my friends. Daniel's visit has left me emotionally exhausted, with that familiar feeling of vulnerability I still can't completely banish. I'm too nervous. Part of me reminds me of everything I've overcome until now and tells me not to be afraid of him. But my body doesn't react the same way.

I decide to go, hiding what happened even from Lucille, who with a single glance has intuited something isn't right. Fortunately, she doesn't press when she sees my smile. Meeting with them at the café, once it's closed to the public, is a weekly plan I don't want to miss.

Gabriela is the last to arrive; I get up to greet her and introduce her to the rest of the group, who immediately resume the conversation as if it had never stopped.

I still can't concentrate enough, so I decide to prepare coffee and some pastries for everyone. These minutes of solitude allow me to breathe and reorganize my thoughts. Though that solitude doesn't last long.

"Is something wrong?" Gabriela's voice startles me, making me spill some of the coffee.

"Shit," I whisper, cleaning everything up.

"It's okay, don't worry," she says, immediately helping me. I try to fill the cup, but my shaking betrays me, and it's too late for her not to notice. "What's wrong, Emma? You're very serious, trembling..."

I glance at the group gathered in the main room, all engrossed in their conversations, completely oblivious to my little crisis. With a discreet gesture, I indicate for Gabriela to follow me to the back room. Once alone, among shelves full of supplies and boxes of books, the words begin to flow:

"My ex was here today," I manage to say, barely looking at her. "It's the second time he's come since I moved, and each time he manages to give me the creeps."

"Did he do anything to you?" she questions, her voice tinged with a mixture of concern and anger. "Because if he touched you, I could..."

"No, he didn't touch me. He doesn't need to in order to hurt me," I let out. This time, tears do overflow my eyes. I've been holding on for too many hours, and it's impossible to contain now.

"Come here," she whispers.

Gabriela wraps her arms around me, embracing me and stroking my back as I release all the fear inside. Her caresses and support help me calm down little by little.

"I won't let that man keep doing this to you," she murmurs, pressing me against her as if wanting to protect me with her entire body. "Didn't you get a restraining order?"

"I wanted to," I explain between sobs, "but his lawyer managed to convince the judge he wasn't a danger to me. Still, just seeing him and..."

"If he shows up again, don't let him near you, and call me. Okay?" she takes my face in her hands. "And call Lucille, and the police if necessary. He knows the power he has over you; that's why he does it, but we won't let him get to you."

"If he sees me calling, it'll be worse..."

She remains thoughtful for a few seconds; I'm sure she's thinking of some alternative to help me, though for now she can't find anything.

"I'll find a solution that will help us, I promise."

Her words and the kiss she leaves on my forehead manage to calm me down. We return to the others, joining the conversation as if neither of us had escaped from it for a few minutes. The only one who notices everything is my best friend, who smiles, making me blush slightly. At this moment, I prefer her to think there was a romantic moment between Gabriela and me rather than having to explain the truth about Daniel.

As the evening progresses, friends begin to leave one by one. Lucille, seeing that Gabriela is staying with me, decides to leave us alone while I close the shop.

"I'll leave you with the pilot," she whispers in my ear as she hugs me. "Don't stay up too late, huh!" she adds with a laugh before disappearing through the door, causing me to shake my head repeatedly.

"She's quite a character," Gabriela comments, smiling, and I mirror her expression.

"She has good intentions, but she's very intense."

"I noticed that," we laugh. "May I walk you home?"

"I live right upstairs," I point just above the café. "I just have to go up the stairs."

"Then my escort duty is already complete," she jokes. I can't help smiling again.

"Would you like to come up?" The words leave my mouth without even thinking them, surprising me.

"I'd truly love to, but I have maneuvers tomorrow, and I'm already running a bit short on time to get back," she pauses briefly; I think she notices the disappointment in my gaze. "But I'd like to meet up and come up with you another day."

"Friday is market day, why don't you join me? I can show you around and maybe cook something delicious afterward."

"That sounds really good," she whispers, and her voice takes on a softer, almost intimate tone. "Well, I have to go. Thanks for the invitation; you have a very welcoming group of friends. They're lovely, though not as much as you," she adds with a wink, making me blush when I hear her. "I'm already looking forward to Friday for our plan."

She moves closer, eliminating any distance between us. She leans in gently to kiss my cheek, making me want much more than that. I think about turning and kissing her lips—those that have been driving me crazy since day one—but I freeze, feeling like an idiot. She smiles, as if she'd heard my thoughts.

"Goodbye, beautiful."

I release all the air in my lungs when she disappears from my sight. I get more nervous every time she's near me, and it becomes harder to contain what I feel inside.

My phone vibrates for the second time in the last few minutes. Two messages from Daniel. I'm not going to let him ruin the peace I have right now, the tranquility that Gabriela has managed to give me. I delete them without even reading them, block him, and enter my home, quickly forgetting about him. I won't let him intimidate me again. Not anymore.

Chapter 6

Gabriela

Workdays stretch long and intense. No rest until the weekend arrives. I welcome it – two days of total freedom that I can use to explore the town and, perhaps, share more time with Emma.

I arrive at the Literary Café a few minutes before our agreed time to pick her up for the market visit. I can't help but close my eyes and breathe deeply when the aroma of freshly brewed coffee hits me the moment I open the door.

"Hello, beautiful," I greet her as she exits the café, finishing pulling on her denim jacket, ready for us to leave. I move closer to give her a kiss on the cheek, and the gesture makes her smile. "How are you?" I ask with a direct look, wanting to know if she's still as nervous as yesterday.

"Better, thanks for caring; you're a sweetheart," she responds, gently stroking my left arm.

"You haven't seen him again, right?"

"No, he sent me a couple of messages last night, but I didn't even open them," she confesses, tugging down on the cuffs of her jacket.

"You did the right thing," I add, taking her chin to look into her eyes. If it were up to me, I'd dive into those red-painted lips that make her even more attractive, if that's possible. "Shall we go?" I offer her my arm, and she takes it instantly as we begin walking toward the market.

For the next two hours, we explore every inch of it. The place is a maze of color and life: wooden stalls with canvas roofs in shades of green and red align in improvised streets. Vendors hawk their wares while street musicians earn coins playing traditional songs. A group of children runs between adults, chasing each other while their parents haggle over prices or select products.

We stop at practically every stall, especially those with local crafts. Emma watches with interest as an old man with strong hands carves figures from pine wood, while I can't take my eyes off a small wolf that seems to observe us as if it were alive.

"To protect the one you love," he tells me with a knowing smile when I buy it and tuck it in my pocket without Emma noticing.

Artisanal cheeses have always been my weakness, and this place seems to have an endless variety. They come in all shapes and colors. With intense or mild flavors. Goat, sheep, cow… a true paradise. And Emma's habit of taking each free sample they offer us and bringing it to my mouth for me to taste makes me tremble, and not from the cold.

A bit later, while she tries to decide between blueberry or wild strawberry jam, I stop to buy a freshly baked loaf of bread. There's something about bread when it's still warm that I can't resist.

"My God, I think we've gone a little overboard, haven't we?" I comment when we reach one of the nearby picnic areas, pulling what we've bought from our bags and placing it on a wooden table.

"Do you really think anything will be left over?" Emma jokes, raising her eyebrows.

"Probably not," I admit, blushing slightly. I'm quite the eater and don't plan to waste a single crumb of what we've brought.

"Besides, if we can't finish something, I'll take it to the café, I'm sure someone will enjoy it," she adds softly.

"I won't let that happen," I tease, licking my lips while staring at each of the delicacies, making her laugh.

The sun shines timidly between clouds, and a cool breeze delights us, enhancing the place. The murmur of people begins to quiet as lunchtime approaches. I'm certain I'll remember this tasting with Emma for the rest of my life. She keeps making me laugh with anecdotes about eccentric café customers, or with stories from her childhood, while offering me bites of different flavors. A bit of aged cheese on bread with virgin olive oil; a piece of caramelized apple that contrasts with blue cheese; a spoonful of pumpkin pie that tastes like autumn. She's much more relaxed; every so often, she moves closer and lets herself be embraced, creating greater closeness and intimacy between us. Sitting beside her was absolutely the right choice.

We finish the tasting with a croissant filled with cream and chocolate, a mixture that spills out when we cut it in two.

"Oh my... That looks so good," I whisper, trying not to drool.

"I've tried the chocolate one, but with the cream mixture, it'll be my first time."

"Then, one bite each at the same time, looking at each other," I add playfully, wanting to savor her expressions while I enjoy this wonder.

"Let's do it…"

Emma starts a countdown from three, laughing continuously, observing my challenging look. When she says "Now!" I open my mouth and take a large piece, larger than I should. Chocolate and cream escape from the corners of my lips, forcing me to put the pastry down on the table and try to control the mess. All this under the watchful gaze of those green eyes, while she laughs at the situation and tries to help me avoid staining myself.

"Wait, let me help you," she whispers, rolling her eyes and shaking her head in amusement.

Her voice sounds distant when her index finger traces my chin and then my lips, cleaning the remains and bringing them to her mouth to enjoy them. That half-smile and her seductive gesture make my core roar and quickly moisten. I run my tongue over my lips, aware that the barrier I was trying to maintain between us has been abandoned in some corner of this market. I try to move closer to kiss her, but a male voice breaks the magic that surrounds us.

"So this is what you're up to…"

Emma's gaze turns sad immediately; she even hides her hands and tenses in her seat. A single second has been enough for me to know it's her idiot ex-husband.

"You didn't answer me last night because you were fucking this one?" he questions, leaving me completely stunned. "So now you like women, huh? That's why you left me."

"I didn't leave you… And everything that happened is your fault, not mine," she counters, not wanting to force her voice. It's clear she's afraid of him.

The man takes a step toward us until he completely invades our space. It's obvious he's trying to intimidate us, but it's not going to work with me. Before he can get any closer, I jump up and position myself between them. I adopt a firm posture, my shoulders straight, my gaze defiant. My attitude seems to amuse him, because he sketches a somewhat stupid smile that turns my stomach.

"Move aside, I want to talk to my wife," he growls.

"Point number one, she's not your wife, you're divorced. Point number two, I don't feel like moving."

"Do you want to make me angry?" he puffs out his chest as if intending to scare me.

"I think you were already angry. And drunk, you reek from here," I shoot back, waving my hand in the air to clear the smell, which makes him even angrier.

"Move!" he yells at me.

"Are you deaf? No, I'm not moving from this spot," I reiterate, adopting a defensive posture in case he tries to attack us.

He stretches his arm, trying to push me in a somewhat clumsy movement. I dodge it, grab his wrist, and twist his forearm, forcing him to turn. He ends up with his back to me, immobilized in a position I can maintain for hours if necessary. He screams and tries to free himself, but each struggle only increases the pressure and pain.

"You see all those people? They're noticing what a despicable being you are. I won't let you get near Emma. And if I find out you do, I assure you this pain will be the minimum I'll inflict. I won't warn you even one more time, is that clear?"

He nods, though I know he's only doing it, so I'll release him, and he won't be further embarrassed. He'll be back; I read it in his face. But I'll be waiting for him.

As he walks away, I glance at Emma out of the corner of my eye as she wipes away the tear tracks that that despicable being has caused.

"Let's get out of here," I whisper, taking her hand. She nods, stands up, and within a few seconds we leave, putting the market behind us.

We don't stop walking until the door to her house closes. I release all the air inside me and, after a few minutes, search for her gaze again. I move a little closer, cradling her face in my hands.

"I'm sorry. I... I didn't want to make a scene, but I wasn't going to let him hurt you again," I apologize, though she immediately shakes her head, momentarily disconcerting me with her reaction.

"Thank you," her voice breaks slightly with emotion. I'm surprised. From her expression, I expected reproaches, embarrassment, maybe even anger, but not gratitude. "Thank you for defending me," she insists. "I don't care what people think; most of them know he only comes to torment me, but nobody stands up to him. And for you to have done it… Whew," she sighs against my neck as she wraps her arms around me in an embrace that leaves me speechless.

I feel how her body fits perfectly with mine. How gradually warmth surrounds us, though we both avoid moving so as not to break the magic of the moment.

"There's only one thing Daniel is right about," she says, sniffling.

"What's that?" I ask, narrowing my eyes, separating just enough to look at her.

"That I like the woman standing in front of me."

Her confession leaves me speechless. I can't even move. She's the one who takes the step, eliminating the small distance between us to join our lips. I close my eyes, feeling her touch. My skin breaks out in goosebumps as the kisses become deeper, and her hands gently tangle in my hair.

I don't know how many minutes we remain like this, kissing, exploring, discovering each other. What I do know is that I desire much more, though at the same time I want to savor each moment, give the time needed to what's growing between us.

As if reading my mind, Emma quickly pulls away, avoiding coming close again no matter how much her body implores it. I can almost see the struggle inside her, I observe it in her eyes, and in part, I understand.

"Are you okay?" I inquire without moving, respecting her space, aware that any misstep could break the fragile trust we've built.

"No… I mean, yes. But this… I don't know how to handle what I'm feeling, Gabriela. I've never been with a woman, and I'm too afraid of getting hurt again."

"I understand," I add to her surprise, keeping calm. "You don't have to say anything else, Emma. But I want you to know one thing," she nods, giving me permission to continue. "I would never hurt you. I know those are words anyone can say, but it's the truth. Though we haven't known each other long, you know that's not my intention with you. I like you, I love the beautiful person I'm getting to know and who stands before me. I know what you need now is a little space to think about everything that's happening. And I'm going to give it to you."

At that moment, I move a little closer to take her hands in mine.

"You'll be the one who takes the next step. When you're ready, and if you want to keep seeing me, let me know. If you don't, absolutely nothing will happen. I understand it's not easy at all."

I leave a goodbye kiss on her cheek before walking out the door without looking back. It's the most responsible and adult decision I could make. I can't decide for her; I know what I feel and what I want, and I won't pressure her into making hasty decisions. She needs to reflect and decide what she wants, and I won't be the one who does it for her.

Chapter 7

Emma

Almost a week has passed since I kissed Gabriela, and seconds later she left. Seven eternal days in which I haven't seen her or heard her voice. I know someday I'll regret not having written even a message, but I think about her last words and know she's right. I'm the one with doubts; I'm the one who needs to take the step.

Since that moment, I can't stop turning the same thoughts over and over. My mind has become a labyrinth with no exit. A vicious circle of questions and doubts from which I can't escape. Yes, I like her, a lot. But she'll leave when her work at the base is done. And then what will happen? What will become of us? Will everything we experience mean nothing? Will they just be painful memories?

I have doubts, so many doubts. Doubts that paralyze me, though my heart screams louder each day to call her. I miss our conversations, those knowing glances, the way her laughter transforms the entire space around her. I miss seeing her appear at the café, watching how she studies the menu even though she always ends up ordering an espresso, feeling that inexplicable sense of peace her mere presence brings me.

"When are you going to call her?"

Lucille's voice pulls me from my thoughts and brings me back to reality. She's drying cups while observing me with that big sister look she's adopted since I told her everything the next morning. And every time she asks that question, my answer is always the same.

"I don't know."

"That indecision of yours will make you lose her," she adds honestly. "Look, I can't speak for you. I know the situation is complicated. But you don't know for certain what will happen. You never know. Yes, her job is temporary, so what? Life can take a thousand turns before that happens. Maybe she'll stay with you, or you'll go with her. But if you don't call her, she'll end up thinking you're not interested, when all three of us know that's not true."

"You think I don't know that?" I question, flustered, setting the knife aside. "I'm being a total coward, Lucille. I'm afraid of losing her, and I don't even have her in my life yet!" my friend's eyes open wide after I yell at her. I take a breath, tears overflow, and I hug her, apologizing. "I'm sorry… I didn't mean to shout. It's just that all this… overwhelms me."

"What are you afraid of?"

"Of falling in love and, when that happens, she leaves," I confess with a long sigh.

"And isn't it simpler to talk about all this with her? To express what you feel and decide together? This only concerns you two, Emma, and it's you two who need to find those answers."

She's right. And I should acknowledge it when she is. At that very moment, I grab my phone and call her, but to my dismay, it's her voicemail that speaks for her: "Major Gabriela Diaz speaking. If you're hearing this message, it means I can't answer you right now. I'll call you as soon as possible."

"Damn…"

"She must be working, don't worry," my best friend whispers beside me. "She'll call you."

"How can you be so sure?"

"Because the sparkle in her eyes every time she looks at you speaks for her."

I decide to take Lucille's advice and not torture myself anymore, at least for the rest of the day. Thanks to customers and work, I manage to distract myself, though I unconsciously can't help checking my phone every few minutes. Morning and afternoon pass in the blink of an eye. I prepare coffees, serve tables, and reorganize several shelves with books newly arrived from the distributor. I function on autopilot until, shortly before closing time, the place empties out. I decide to close early; the weekend will be intense, and these extra minutes will give me a small breather. With everything put away and the lights off, I step outside and prepare to lock up.

"Well... I think I arrived a little late."

Her voice makes my stomach flutter with excitement. I look at her and inevitably smile seeing her in front of me. She does too.

"I thought I wouldn't see you today..."

"I saw your call right after landing, it's been an exhausting day, and I thought about staying to rest. But when I reached the base, I realized what I needed most was to see you and spend some time with you."

What do you say when the words you hear from the person you're dying to see are exactly what you wanted to hear? A simple, silly smile appears on my face.

"Have you had dinner?" I ask without thinking too much.

"No."

"Want to come up? I'll prepare something tasty, and we can talk quietly."

"I'd love to," she admits with a beautiful smile.

I use the time it takes to lock up and climb the stairs to ask about her work. She responds with light anecdotes, avoiding technical details she knows I wouldn't understand. In turn, she questions me about how the week at the café has gone. The conversation flows naturally for the next few minutes, but when we finally sit down to dinner, the atmosphere changes and seriousness settles in my tone of voice.

"I need to talk about what happened," I suddenly say, wanting to release everything I feel.

"Me too, Emma. It's been some very strange days," she acknowledges, nodding her head slowly.

"I haven't stopped thinking about the kiss, our conversations, the moments we spend together..."

"And what is it you want to ask?" It's clear she reads my thoughts.

"What will happen when your work at the base ends?"

Her sigh confirms to me that this isn't easy for her either and that, perhaps, she's also spent sleepless nights turning the matter over.

"I don't know, Emma. Normally, I'd go back home, but since I met you, that's what I least want to do," she admits, continuing to look at me. "My future is always uncertain with the job I have, that's why my relationships don't last. They never understand the sacrifice I make, and, for the first time in my life, I have someone in front of me who does. But I know you wouldn't leave your café behind for me, nor would I let you do it," she reflects. "What I mean is that, despite what may come, I want to continue getting to know you and, if you give me the chance, try. I know I'm making this very complicated for you, I have no doubt, but I know you understand the reasons behind it."

"Yes…" I sigh, taking a sip from my glass. "I've seen firsthand the sacrifices you make. And I understand them too."

"All we can do, without knowing what the future holds, is let ourselves be carried by the situation and the moment."

"Live what life brings us without thinking about what will happen…"

"Yes, but only if you're willing to do so. I'm not going to force you to do it. It's difficult to get to know someone knowing that, maybe, they might leave your life when you least expect it. But if we don't try, we won't even know what we're missing."

"Would we be exclusive?" I ask, aware that something might come up at the base or outside of it during this time.

"Do you want me all to yourself, miss?" she questions back, playfully.

"Is that asking too much?" I blush seeing how she approaches, positioning herself between my legs, and takes my hands before pressing her forehead to mine.

"No, it's not," she whispers, leaving a kiss on the tip of my nose, causing tingles throughout my body. "Are you completely sure about this? I know you like to have everything under control, and this won't be..."

"To be honest, I know it's going to be hard, and I'll doubt... but it's just..." my gaze runs up and down her.

"But it's just, what?"

"It's impossible to resist," I blurt out before grabbing her waist and pulling her close to me again, joining our lips this time for a new kiss. One very different from the previous one. A soft and calm one, more romantic, that unites us even more.

And the only thing I'm clear about is that each day she drives me even crazier.

Chapter 8

Gabriela

Since our dinner a couple of nights ago, things with Emma have only improved. After each of my shifts, the routine is always the same: I take a good shower, swap my uniform for civilian clothes, and rush out to see her. I'm aware that some of the personnel exchange smiles when they see me dart out or when I return in the early morning with slightly tousled hair and a smile impossible to hide. Some even dare to make comments under their breath, but one look is enough to silence them immediately. The funny thing is that it doesn't even bother me anymore; I'm beginning to fully accept this new life I'm building away from the sky.

Today I have the afternoon completely free, and Emma has suggested visiting the town gardens, a place that, according to her, is magical at sunset. As I push open the café door, the bell tinkles, announcing my arrival, and I find her chatting with Lucille, who greets me from a distance, and I return the gesture with a friendly nod.

"Weren't you going to close the café?" I ask with a smile when she approaches me.

"That was the plan, but when I told Lucille, she said she'd take care of it," her voice drops a bit, taking on a confidential tone. "She likes spending time here. She's doing me a favor, and it's extra money for her. Though I suspect she mainly does it to see us leave together," she explains, amused, as we look at her. When she returns our gaze, we laugh and make her blush.

We leave the café laughing—that kind of happiness that emerges when you feel completely comfortable with someone. The afternoon sun bathes the cobblestone streets of Zelenova, while in a corner, a couple of lazy cats stretch out seeking the last rays of sunlight. We love this game of teasing with Lucille; somehow I feel it helps us get to know each other a bit more and builds her trust in me.

We walk for the next few minutes, sharing details of our day. I tell her about this morning's flight session, omitting classified details but describing the freedom I feel when the sky opens before me. Emma listens attentively, as if my words were a book she can't put down. She tells me about the parade of characters who've passed through the café: from the history professor who always sits at the same table by the window, to a group of Chinese tourists trying to decipher the drink menu.

When we reach the gardens, words disappear. It's a comfortable silence, one of those reverent silences caused by the beauty surrounding us. She's spoken highly of this place, but seeing it up close is much more incredible. The garden is an explosion of colors and shapes. Paths that wind between beds of wildflowers. Old oak trees extending their branches as if wanting to greet you, small ponds where water reflects the sunset light.

"Do you like it?" she asks, softly grabbing my arm.

"I love it," I sigh. "I think I'll come here more than I imagined, especially if this peace and tranquility can be breathed every day."

"I assure you it's like this. When I have time and can spare a moment, I grab a book and come read here. The sunset is incredible; I didn't want you to miss something like that," she adds, resting her head on my shoulder.

"Thank you for bringing me," I say gratefully, before leaving a kiss on her cheek.

We walk the paths calmly, as if we had all the time in the world. Emma guides me through the areas she likes most, pointing out a particularly beautiful rose or a hidden corner. From time to time, our hands brush, sending small electric shocks through my fingers. The sun shines down, giving us the warmth and peace we both sought. When we finish our walk, we find a perfect spot under an old tree where sun and shade compete. We place the blanket on the grass and sit to rest and enjoy the moment.

"This is truly wonderful," I admit in a whisper, letting myself fall completely onto the blanket. Emma lies down beside me, and I can't help looking at her and smiling. "I like this…"

"Me too," she confesses with a smile to die for.

My fingers gently caress the back of her hand, even timidly. Her smile and her hand intertwining with mine confirm that I'm not the only one comfortable with this closeness. So while she strokes my knuckles with her thumb, I take the opportunity to bring up a topic I wanted to propose.

"Do you have anything to do tomorrow night?" I ask, trying to maintain a casual tone.

"If you mean after closing the café, I don't have plans. Why do you ask?"

"Some colleagues from the base are meeting for drinks, kind of informal. If you'd like, you can come..."

"Won't I be in the way there?"

"No," I hasten to respond. "Colleagues from various departments are coming with their partners and friends; it's just socializing," Seeing Emma's indecision, I decide to continue. "I don't have such a close-knit group of friends as you do, but I'd love for you to meet Ghost and the people I have around me in my daily life."

"Do they know that you...?"

"No, they don't know anything about my personal life. And this isn't to affirm anything or anything like that. It's simply because I enjoy sharing my time with you, and I want you to know more about me just as I do about you."

"That's very sweet, Gabriela... I'll be delighted to accompany you."

I think the sparkle in my eyes is more than enough to make her smile. I'm excited, even if we're just two women getting to know each other.

"I should warn you that my behavior with them will be more rigid and serious than what you know. I'm different at the base."

"You're their superior, I understand that. And don't worry, nothing you might do or say will scare me off."

Her confidence and certainty makes me feel at peace, especially after these kinds of conversations that fill me like they never have before. I sit up, leaning on my left arm, coming close to her. I gently caress her face, tracing the line of her jaw with my fingertips and, when she closes her eyes, captive to relaxation itself, I join my lips with hers. It's a soft, tender kiss, full of love. One of her hands holds my neck, preventing me from pulling away, making me smile before continuing to kiss her for a few more seconds. When I pull back, she sighs, making me laugh.

"Are you okay?" I inquire without moving away.

"Better than ever, Gabriela. The peace and tranquility I feel with you is so new and so comforting..."

"That's very good. And I feel the same way, that's why whenever I can and have free time, I spend it with you. You make me feel at home," I admit, surprising her, "and I don't think I've ever felt this way with anyone."

The word "home" has a special meaning for me. For someone like me, who has lived her entire life on military bases around the world, admitting that I've found a home in a person is something very special.

The silence that follows my words is revealing. There's fear in both of us, I can feel it: fear of the intensity of what's growing between us, fear of the unknown, fear of how vulnerable this feeling makes us. But there's also a desire to move forward, to explore the future of our relationship together. And here we are, launching ourselves, letting ourselves be carried by what we feel and by the opportunities that come our way. I think we're on the right path, and I'm sure neither of us is going to waste everything that life gives us.

Chapter 9

Emma

My reception at the base proved less intimidating than I'd imagined. Knowing that no one knew the details of Gabriela's private life kept me especially alert. It forced me to pay attention to every interaction, every gesture, every unspoken word. Even more so when I met Ghost—his looks told me he wasn't sure what was happening but that he'd figure it out eventually. She remained confident with the rest of the personnel. Everyone respected her, and she had no reservations about introductions. They treated her with respect that went beyond her rank; a mixture of admiration and trust. Still, she didn't let me stay alone for even a second, especially knowing how nervous I was. She discreetly touched my back to reassure me if she saw I was tense at any moment or if the pilots' technical jargon left me lost.

Now, twenty-four hours later, I'm very glad I accepted her invitation. Getting to know that less personal side also thrills me. It's like unveiling a new facet of this woman who gradually occupies each of my thoughts.

"Well, that's it, I think I'm done here," Lucille announces, approaching after finishing cleaning the last tables. "Do you need anything else?"

"No, thanks for coming and giving me a hand. I wanted everyone to be served as well as possible, and two hands weren't enough."

"You know it's a pleasure to help you, friend. Are you closing now?"

"Yes, I'll clean this up and go. Get going before the rain gets heavier."

With a smile and a kiss on the cheek, she rushes home. A big storm was expected, and it's already reaching us. The sky has turned a threatening leaden gray, and the first lightning bolts briefly illuminate the empty streets. Luckily, I only have to climb a few steps—it won't catch me. I finish closing the register, turn off the lights, and go out. The wind is unbearable, but I manage to lower the gate and lock up. I'm about to go upstairs when a familiar silhouette catches my attention under the now torrential rain. I wait two seconds and can make her out perfectly:

"Where do you think you're going with this rain?" I shout, seeing her completely soaked. "Come in!" I shout, opening the door to let her in ahead of me.

"The rain caught me halfway, and I decided to keep going," she explains, shrugging.

"Gabriela, you're drenched." Instinctively, my hands move to her face, removing a strand of hair that had stuck to it. "You're going to catch a cold. Come on, let's go upstairs."

It takes only seconds to climb the stairs. I send her straight to the shower to warm up and avoid a cold. Meanwhile, I look for some clothes to give her and clean up the trail of water she's left on the floor. When I have everything, I enter the bathroom.

"Here are some clothes, and a towel so you can dry yourself."

I try not to look through the shower door, but this woman is like a magnet, and I can't help it. Her figure is perfectly visible. Could this moment seem any more sensual?

"Thanks, beautiful."

"If you need anything, let me know," I add, somewhat nervously.

I rush out, trying to calm my nerves. If being near her causes this tangle of feelings, seeing her naked multiplies it by a million. I decide not to think about it and start cooking while she finishes, though I can't quite concentrate knowing she's showering naked just a few feet away.

When the door opens, and I see her appear with just a towel, I nearly drop the utensils from my hands. Luckily, a reflex prevents it.

"Sorry, Emma, do you have a wider T-shirt? With the shower I've warmed up, and I won't be able to stand the sweater for long."

I swallow, trying to make my voice sound natural, though I can't look away.

"Sure, come on, I'll find you one."

She follows me to the bedroom. I quickly search the closet and find one that will work. I nod with a smile and, before I realize it, I see her letting her towel drop to dress right there. My head at that moment tells me to turn around to give her privacy, or to leave and let her alone. However, my eyes remain trapped on her naked body and, shortly after, on her gaze, the one that floods me, leaving me ecstatic and paralyzed.

There are no words, only actions. Gabriela stands up without finishing dressing, with only tiny black panties covering her body. She crosses the room and the few feet that separate us, finding my waist and my lips with urgency. They are soft and warm, she explores mine, causing my underwear to soak through. I surround her with my arms, pulling her close and caressing her skin, fitting our bodies together for the first time.

At any other moment, I would be more nervous. Even so, her confidence transmits calm to me, and I let myself be carried away and guided by her at all times. I gasp against her mouth as she undresses me little by little, letting each piece of clothing fall at our feet. She does it with haste, with hunger. My fingers continue playing with her skin, growing hotter. She pushes me slightly, and we fall onto my bed, with desperate kisses and much-desired caresses. Each touch, each sigh, each moan—it's a game we don't want to end. The storm roars outside, but in here it ceases to exist, giving way to the sound of our kisses, our ragged breathing, and our moans.

Gabriela slides over my body, leaving a trail of wet kisses along my neck and collarbone, making me tremble each time her teeth graze my shoulder. I arch my back as her hands glide across my torso. Her hips and mine begin a more than pleasurable game, moving up and down, giving us what we've been craving. She pauses for a second to finish undressing me and remove what little clothing she had left. She kisses me again, leaving me breathless, and a new gasp makes her smile.

Her fingers descend down my body until they reach my sex, completely wet. She looks at me, checking that I'm comfortable and, somehow, asking for permission. A simple nod of my head is all the answer she needs. She enters me, causing a moan to escape that resonates between the four walls surrounding us. She holds my body, enjoying my being and every spasm that runs through me. She encircles my neck with her free hand, staying close to me while her fingers begin to move at a perfect rhythm.

I feel how pleasure accumulates in my lower abdomen—a growing pressure that threatens to overflow at any moment. I open my eyes, and the smile she gives me when she understands I'm about to have an orgasm makes me tremble.

"Enjoy it to the end, beautiful," she whispers in my ear.

One of her fingers caresses my clitoris, giving me even more pleasure, while two others continue inside me, wetting her hand. Unable to hold on any longer, I release everything I've been holding in and delight in what I've just felt. It's not my first sexual experience, though it is with a woman, with her, and it's been much more intense than I could have ever imagined.

My body falls spent onto the sheets, every muscle relaxed. Recovering my breath and some of the strength I've left on that sheet.

"Are you okay?" she asks me, caressing my cheek with the back of her hand.

"More than okay," I whisper. "It was incredible."

She smiles before kissing me. I try to sit up while still kissing her, though she stops me for a moment, having seen my intentions.

"You don't have to…"

"I want to, Gabriela. And I want you to do it to me again afterward," she smiles again. "I've been wanting this since the first moment I saw you."

"That means…"

"That I don't plan to let you sleep all night," I joke before pushing her and straddling her.

The rest of the night comes down to one orgasm after another until our bodies can't take any more. The only thing I can think when I end up resting on her chest is that I don't want to wake from this wonderful dream and that, for nothing in the world, would I want to lose her.

Chapter 10

Gabriela

The sun streams through the curtains of Emma's bedroom, and I savor the view, though I've been doing so for an hour already. The maneuvers at the base happen at dawn, programming my body like a Swiss watch. I can't sleep past that hour, not even on days off like today.

Her naked body with sheets tangled at her waist—that peaceful, happy face is all I needed to start the day in the best possible way, and it has finally happened. I rise carefully to avoid waking her, and pad barefoot to the kitchen, searching for what I need to prepare breakfast. I make some toast and coffee, plus slice a small bowl of fruits from her refrigerator.

Suddenly, I hear soft footsteps approaching timidly. Perhaps anyone else wouldn't have heard them, but I have so many stimuli in my work that I've trained all my senses never to fail me.

"Good morning," Emma whispers, hugging me from behind and leaving a kiss on my neck as soft as the flutter of a butterfly's wings, but which sends electric currents throughout my spine.

"Good morning," I respond, glancing at her with a smile.

"Isn't it very early?" she asks, resting her cheek against my shoulder.

"Yeah, sorry if I woke you. I'm incapable of sleeping past seven in the morning," I explain while continuing to prepare the coffee. "It's like having an internal alarm clock I can't turn off."

"It's okay; I usually get up early too, though I don't open until ten," she responds, and I can feel her smile against my skin. "Are you working today?"

"No, do you have any plans?"

"For now, staying hugged to you while you finish breakfast. I could get used to this..."

"You shouldn't."

"Why?" she questions in a more serious tone. "Don't you like being here?"

"I love it, Emma, and I wish I could do it every day of the week," I sigh as I set down what I have in my hands and cradle her face before continuing. "I say it because my work starts at six thirty in the morning, and by this time I wouldn't be here to make you breakfast," her expression relaxes when she hears me; I think I scared her. "Though I'd always try to leave coffee made for you or some sweet in the oven. Sorry if I made you think something else..."

"No, it's okay," she soothes, closing her eyes and letting herself be embraced. "I just like this so much that I forget you have responsibilities."

"I know, it's fine. We'll make the most of every moment I have free when they don't need me," I assure her before kissing her. "Today, if you'd like, I can help you at the café... My first job was as a barista, at 18. It'll be nice to remember old times."

"Are you sure you want to spend your day off working with me?" she inquires, arching her eyebrows in surprise and unable to suppress a smile.

"It sounds like a fantastic plan, honestly," I admit, confident. "But first... breakfast and shower, I need it."

"Now that's an awesome plan," she affirms, biting her lower lip.

We sit on the kitchen stools, side by side, our shoulders brushing with each movement. We savor everything I've prepared and chat about everything and nothing; about our days and all we'd like to do in the future. We speak in plural, both of us, as we want to do all that hand in hand, though we don't really know if one day it will happen.

As soon as we finish, we tidy the bedroom, and before I know it, she sheds her pajamas and runs naked to the shower, causing me to do the same. I end up embracing and kissing her in the small cubicle.

"Are you teasing me again?" I question, nibbling at her neck, noticing how the hair on her nape stands on end.

"M-maybe," she responds, stifling a moan in her throat while squeezing my buttocks firmly.

"You learn fast, huh?"

Merging our bodies under the shower is too tempting. The doubts, fears, indecisions… everything gets diluted and washed away with the water that disappears down the drain. The shower extends much longer than planned, and when we finally run out of energy, we collapse sitting on the bathtub floor, with water still falling on us. We look at each other and laugh; patience isn't our strong suit in these situations.

We open the café minutes before the scheduled time. Emma has lent me a black apron that contrasts with my white t-shirt, and soon I find myself naturally performing the tasks she entrusts to me, demonstrating my past skills as a barista. I realize it's like riding a bike—you don't forget, no matter how many years pass. The morning goes by with furtive glances, the occasional kiss in the stockroom, and many customers curious about my presence there, who keep staring at me.

We're laughing about those looks when my phone vibrates insistently in my pocket. I take it out and see the screen lit up with the number I would recognize even in my sleep: a call from the base. I feel my face transform in a matter of seconds. This can only mean one thing: work.

Emma notices immediately.

"Everything okay?" she asks, seeing my change of expression.

"I have an urgent meeting and need to leave right away," I explain, shrugging apologetically as I put the phone back in my pocket.

"You have to go? Now?"

"Yes." I look at her and know she doesn't like this, neither do I. "It's a new mission, we leave tonight."

"But how long will you be gone?"

"I don't know," I admit as I remove the apron and hand it to her. "It'll take days, or even weeks. Damn..."

"Will we at least be able to talk?"

"Probably not. They'll cut communications as soon as we arrive," observing the sadness in her eyes, I take her hand and lead her to the stockroom. "I know this is unexpected, that it might be a short or long time, especially now that our thing... well, is just beginning. But I can't refuse. I have to go. Not being able to talk to you or see you daily will be absolute hell, Emma, but I'll try to come back as soon as possible, okay?"

Her tears run down her cheeks without saying a word.

"Promise me you'll take care of yourself, and that you'll come back safe and sound," she whispers as she wipes them with her shirt sleeve.

"I always do, this time won't be different, beautiful," I assure her, drying one of her tears with my thumb. "Especially having such a wonderful woman waiting for me."

Our gazes meet one last time. I kiss her calmly before leaving without looking back. I know that if I do, I won't be able to go, and I must follow orders.

Emma

My heart shatters watching Gabriela leave. I follow her out, wiping away tears and watching her retreat down the cobblestone street until she turns a corner and vanishes from my sight. I don't even know how to feel. I lean against the large window, facing the sun, trying to calm myself before going back inside.

"Emma?" Lucille's voice brings me back to reality after a few seconds. "What's wrong? Why are you crying?"

While she hugs me, I tell her everything that happened from when Gabriela arrived last night until this very moment. My words tumble out, mixing with sobs I can't contain. She tightens her embrace even more when she realizes that what I feel for this woman grows stronger each day.

"She'll be back," she assures me, smiling and squeezing my hands between hers to encourage me.

"What if something happens to her? What if...?" I can't even finish the sentence.

"Don't expect the worst, friend. We know she's one of the best. She'll come back. And when she does, you should talk to her."

"Talk about what?"

"About how in love you are, about the two of you..."

She's right; she always is. I should tell her about my feelings, about what I want... about what I fear. But until then, the wait will be eternal.

Chapter 11

Emma

Two weeks. It's been two weeks already, and I know nothing about her. I haven't stopped thinking about Gabriela for a single moment. During work hours at the café, while I take orders and recommend books, her image constantly slips into my head. At night, the bed feels too large, too empty without her. And the silence... the silence only amplifies her absence. The only thing I've confirmed amid all my doubts is how much I miss her and how in love I am. Even though we're going with the flow and things seem good between us, I still have my fears. And I know she knows it.

The café and the people who visit it daily are my life. My best friend and this town are all I have. Maybe it doesn't seem like much, but to me, it's everything. And thinking that Gabriela might never become part of it makes me so sad. Lucille comes every day and accompanies me as much as she can during the long workdays. She sits at the counter while I prepare coffees or helps with orders when the place fills up. Though I thank her from the bottom of my heart, her presence doesn't fill the void Gabriela has left. It's like trying to illuminate a huge dark room with a match: it helps, but it's not enough.

After another sigh, she puts down what she's holding and comes to my side.

"What are you thinking about?" she asks, though we both know the answer very well.

"About her," I admit, wiping the countertop with a cloth. "It's all I've thought about since she left."

"I've never seen you like this over anyone..."

"Because I've never felt something so strong for someone, Luci," I confess with a sigh, dropping the cloth. "I was attracted to her from the first moment, the connection we have is… incredible. I can't even imagine a future without her."

"Wow, she hit the bullseye."

"And hard," I admit, leaning on the counter with both elbows. "The worst part is not knowing anything about her. Having no news. Not even knowing if she's okay. If we could at least talk or send messages..."

"And that's very understandable. The fear that something might happen to her is greater," I nod. Her support and understanding ease the burden a little.

The café door opens again, and my friend moves to attend to the customer to give me a few minutes of peace, but the woman says my name, catching my attention.

"Hi, Melissa," I greet her, surprised. "What brings you here?"

"Haven't you checked your email?"

"My… my email? No," I shake my head, feeling my heart begin to beat faster. "What's happening? Has something happened to her?" I immediately grab my phone while I listen to her speak.

"The mission is over. They're all coming home safe and sound. I thought you knew!"

My fingers tremble as I refresh the email app. And there it is, a brief message that makes my entire body shiver:

Hello, beautiful.

We're coming home. Yes, I'm fine, a bit bruised, but safe and sound. See you soon.

Love you, Gabriela.

Tears are already running down my cheeks before I can stop them. My friend hugs me, and I quickly grasp Melissa's hands, who smiles as gratefully as I am. In this moment, we both share the same relief. They're coming home.

"You'll come to the reception, right?"

"Reception?" I repeat, confused.

"Yes, it's a small informal party we prepare for them after such a long mission. Partners and friends come and welcome them back as they deserve."

I feel heat rising to my cheeks when I hear the word "partner."

"I don't know if it's appropriate... I..." I stammer, unsure.

"You're a good... friend of Gabriela's, aren't you?" she adds, emphasizing the word friend with a wink. "At the last gathering she looked very happy with your presence, and we thought she'd like to have you there when she arrives," she adds, making my heart skip several beats as I listen.

I think about it for a few seconds. I know the people who will be there will be the partners of the group. So they suspect that we are a couple. Has Gabriela told them or confirmed something? Before I lose myself in my thoughts, I nod and confirm my attendance. Within seconds, she passes me the invitation and asks me to be at the base two hours before the group arrives tomorrow, to prepare their welcome.

As soon as Melissa leaves the café, Lucille sticks close to me again and hugs me, giving me that smile that screams, "I told you so."

"Something tells me all those people suspect you're a couple," she comments, shrugging.

"Yes, I got the same impression," I sigh, biting my lower lip.

"Are you?" she questions, doubtful.

"I don't even know myself," I admit. "We decided to let what we're experiencing flow, and if the moment came, make it official. But with all this mission stuff, it was put on hold."

"Well, only one day until you can clear up your doubts and talk to her about it."

***

I arrive at Melissa and Rick's house with a box of homemade sweets that I prepare for the café. Today's batch turned out delicious, and I'm sure everyone will love them. As soon as she sees me arrive, Melissa greets me with a smile and a hug. She introduces me to some people I haven't met yet, and immediately, we continue with the preparations they've already started.

"Do you know what time they'll arrive?" I ask her without stopping arranging things.

"In less than an hour, more or less. It's usually always the same time, even if they don't say anything. It's the group's customs and quirks."

"I understand," I add with a smile.

"It's the first time Gabriela has someone waiting for her," Chari, a woman in her forties with red-dyed hair, joins us and comments, looking at me with curiosity. "She doesn't usually stay long at the receptions, but with you here I'm sure she will."

Her gestures are knowing; it's clear they believe we're a couple. It's more than evident.

"So, she never stays?" I ask, feeling curious to learn more about this facet of Gabriela.

"Just for a short while. Only to say hello," Melissa responds. "She's quite reserved. That's why we were so surprised when she came accompanied last time."

"Well, it was… it was something informal," I respond a bit nervously, feeling the heat rise to my cheeks. "She asked me for a favor, and I accepted."

"We know. But the fact that she did it for the first time already means something," Chari says before walking away with a tray of canapés in her hands.

I watch her as she walks away, not knowing what to say. Melissa's gaze makes me release all the air I've been holding in. She immediately realizes I'm uncomfortable and doesn't hesitate to pull me slightly away from the others to talk privately.

"Sorry we're so direct," she says, lowering her voice. "We're just happy that Gabriela has someone…"

"I know, it's just…" I take her by the arm and pull her a bit further away, making sure no one can hear us. "There's… there's still nothing clear between us. And the fact that everyone is assuming, well…"

"I understand, and I hope you'll forgive us. We thought it was already official."

"No, but to tell you the truth, I hope it will be soon." We look at each other and smile. No more words are needed.

Together, in a matter of minutes, the welcome party is prepared, and all we have to do is wait for the pilots to arrive. Melissa and Rick's garden looks beautiful, with lights hanging between the trees, tables arranged with white tablecloths, and flowers in small glass vases. Soft jazz music plays from speakers camouflaged among the bushes. Everything has a homey and welcoming air.

The conversation with the rest of the group flows easily, and they don't mention anything more about the relationship that might exist between Gabriela and me, which I appreciate. I feel that the group is becoming a good friendship that can last a long time, and that's something I love. They're pleasant, very optimistic, and hardworking. I hope we can repeat these kinds of situations much more often.

Almost at the expected time, a convoy of SUVs arrives and parks at the door. Some of the women go out, and others, like me, prefer to wait inside. Especially me, since I'm not expected to be here and it might be a pleasant surprise, or so I hope.

Chapter 12

Gabriela

Today, more than ever, coming home fills me with a sense of relief and joy I've never experienced before. The adrenaline of the mission has faded away, giving way to a deeper, more personal emotion. And it's Emma who occupies every one of my thoughts since we received the order to return. Her face, her smile, her green eyes have been my anchor during these two weeks.

I always considered these missions as the fundamental part of my job. The danger, the constant tension, the responsibility of making decisions in split seconds... Everything was as natural to me as breathing. However, this time has been very different. It took me an eternity to take off from the Zelenova runway, as if an invisible part of my own being had remained anchored to this place... or to her.

My silences throughout the mission were longer and deeper than usual. The squadron noticed, though nobody said anything directly, but it was clear in many of the looks Ghost threw my way during briefings, as if he could read on my face what was happening to me. I keep wondering how those with family and children continue risking their lives day after day, knowing that the best part of their lives waits for them at home.

"Come on, Gabi, you have to come!" Ghost's pleas bring me back to the real world. "Come to my house. Melissa and the others will have prepared some party for our arrival. It's our ritual! You can't miss it."

"You won't stop insisting until I say yes, will you?"

"Obviously," he adds, raising his eyebrows with an almost theatrical gesture, knowing I'll accept without much choice.

I do, but with very little enthusiasm. All I want right now is a hot shower and then to rush to Emma's café, not socialize with the group at a welcome party that I always attend merely out of courtesy.

Little by little, all the cars enter the base and stop around Rick and Melissa's house. Reaper lifts his wife and spins her around while their young children run around them laughing. Shadow kisses his wife as if they'd been separated for years instead of two weeks. Other couples melt into long embraces and some tears. Their happiness invades me for a moment and makes me smile. Melissa approaches and hugs me.

"Don't tell me you're leaving!" I look at Ghost—he's played me again.

"I'll just stay for a bit, I… want to go rest."

"Yeah, I don't think you'll feel the same when you see her," she takes my arm without letting me say anything more.

She pulls me into the house. And, as if by magnetic force, my eyes stop on her. She's talking to another attendee but, as soon as she sees me, she politely excuses herself and approaches. By her laugh, I know I must look stupid, still rooted to the same spot. The last thing I expected was to find her here.

"I'm happy to see you too," she says, smiling at my dumbfounded face before hugging me.

I close my eyes feeling her body embracing mine. All the tension, all the fatigue, the pressure of leading the squadron, disappear instantly. I don't know how she does it, but she always manages to make me feel better.

"But, what are you doing here?" I ask, confused.

We both move slightly away from the group; we know they're watching us, so we try to maintain our posture and pretend, as much as we want to devour each other with kisses as soon as possible.

"Melissa came to the café two days ago. She told me about the email you'd sent—with all the work I hadn't even seen it. And she asked me to be here," she leans in to whisper. "They assume there's something between us," she adds, alternating glances between them and me. "So I said yes. I was so eager to see you that I couldn't wait much longer."

"I was also really eager to come back, Emma," I sigh, hugging her again. "Ghost insisted a lot that I come, so I guess they had it well planned."

We look for them with our eyes. Immediately, they stop watching us and pretend, a gesture that makes us smile.

"Maybe we should talk and clarify things between us, don't you think?" she asks, raising her eyebrows.

"Yes... How about if I go to your apartment in a couple of hours? I'd like to take a shower and put on something more comfortable."

"Sure, change at your own pace, and I'll wait for you there."

We approach Rick and Melissa to say goodbye. This time, they don't stop us; they know we need to be together. The others don't even notice we're leaving. I ask Emma to go ahead and wait for me at the door, taking the opportunity to talk to them:

"Thank you for inviting her," I thank Melissa heartfelt.

"She's a sweetheart, and she'll always be welcome in the group," she assures with a smile and a wink that makes me laugh.

The only thing I can think about is that I have more people around me who care than I imagined.

***

Not even an hour has passed when I'm crossing her threshold and our bodies unite without saying a single word. Our kisses, desperate and hungry, say everything that words cannot. We move blindly, guided only by desire, until my legs hit the sofa. We fall onto the cushions without separating our lips, tangled in an embrace that tries to make up for two weeks of separation.

"I've missed you so much," Emma whispers, hiding her face in my neck. I feel the wetness of her tears against my skin and realize that mine are also flowing freely down my cheeks.

"And I've missed you, beautiful. So much," I respond, hugging her tightly.

"Will it always be like this? Without communication, without being able to talk even for a few minutes?"

I pull back slightly to look into her eyes while I caress her hair, letting the strands slip through my fingers.

"No, it depends on how confidential the mission is and how focused they need us to be. For strategic and secret missions, we establish a routine where technology doesn't enter. It's for security. If they intercept any communication, it could become very dangerous."

"I understand… but it's so hard," she murmurs against my shoulder.

"It had never been so difficult for me," I admit with a sigh. "I'm always the only one with no one waiting for her when we return. Everyone has a wife and children. But I… Many times I've even wondered how they risk so much when something as wonderful as family waits for them at home, not knowing if they'll return alive or not."

"It's not easy," she confesses, wiping her tears with the palm of her hand. "But it's your profession, your passion. And only the people who love you come to understand it."

I look at her, smile, and the word luck returns to my mind. I don't know if it's a beautiful coincidence or the greatest fortune that could happen to me; the only thing I know and am clear about is that I want this every day of my life.

"Do you love me?" I ask her, not taking my eyes off her.

"Yes, I've fallen in love with you," she blurts without thinking. "And during these two weeks, it's become even clearer. I think if you'd been gone a little longer, Lucille would have ended up dragging me by the hair because of how annoying I was."

We laugh, and she immediately tells me everything that has happened in these two weeks. How she felt, how her best friend didn't leave her side for a single day, the sleepless nights worried about whether I was okay… And, after a comfortable silence, the moment comes that I think we were both waiting for.

"I know it will be complicated with the missions, with my job in general," I whisper, sitting up straight. She follows me instantly, her knees brushing against mine. "But I want to be with you, to share everything with you. I want to be able to sleep by your side every day, even if I have to wake up even earlier to return to the base."

"We can sleep there too, at your place," she adds, making me smile. "I want to as well, Gabriela. I won't be able to help worrying every time you have to leave, but I want to do it, I want to be with you, to keep moving forward. And whatever comes in the future, we'll overcome it together."

"Are you completely sure?"

"As sure as you and I are here in this moment."

Our lips seek each other with urgency. There are no hesitations anymore, no uncertainties, just the certainty that this is right. I slide my fingers across her cheek, leaning even closer to her, feeling how she stifles a moan in her throat when the kiss becomes more passionate. With an agile movement, I stand up and sit astride her legs. Our bodies fit perfectly, and the heat becomes increasingly suffocating. Emma's hands travel down my back, gently scratching each of my muscles beneath my clothes, igniting small fires wherever they pass. At last we are one. Just us and the night that begins to arrive, enveloping us in its intimacy.

She begins to unbutton my shirt, removing it immediately, in a hurry. I moan against her lips when she squeezes my breasts, giving me instant pleasure. I smile before continuing to kiss her while I explore her body with my hands, removing clothes and memorizing again every inch of her skin.

"I've missed you so much," she whispers as I move down her neck, kissing and licking it as I please.

I lay her down completely and continue my journey, delighting in her chest and skin, which bristles at my passage, until I reach her sex. Her underwear is wet; her left hand holding my head gives me enough permission to make her scream with pleasure, which I do immediately.

For the next few minutes, her moans and sighs are the only sounds heard within these four walls. I just hope she has enough strength because I plan to lose myself in her body all night, again and again, until she can't take anymore.

Chapter 13

Emma

Days begin to pass, and you could say that Gabriela and I are starting our new life together. Whenever she's not on duty or during moments when the bookstore isn't too hectic, we spend time together. Her presence has become as natural in my life as the scent of freshly brewed coffee in the mornings. On her days off, she settles into my home and becomes one more fixture in the café. People are getting used to her presence, and I love that.

She sits in her usual corner by the window, with a book in her hands and a cup of American coffee that I refill without her asking. Occasionally, when the place is quiet, I catch her watching me work, with that intense gaze that makes me blush like a teenager. Seeing her chat with some of the town's elderly about military history gives me a feeling I can't describe.

On days she has work, she spends the night in my apartment. She slides under the sheets after a quick shower and hugs me as if she wants to melt into me.

Except when she's really pressed for time; then I'm the one who goes to the base right after closing the café, or I even allow myself to close early to gain a few extra minutes with her.

Everything has become so normalized between us and the people around us that I've even experienced some amusing anecdotes. Though what I'll never forget are the questions and laughs from Mr. Johansen, my neighbor in the adjacent apartment. He's an old man in his eighties, with a perfectly trimmed white beard and blue eyes that still retain a wonderful sparkle.

More than once, just after leaving home, I've found him leaning on his carved wooden cane, waiting by the entrance as if anticipating a conversation.

"And your friend?" he asks with a mischievous smile that multiplies the wrinkles around his eyes.

"Gabriela?" I respond, though we both know perfectly well who he's referring to. He nods quickly, tapping the floor gently with his cane. "She's working. She left early."

"That I know," he says, leaning slightly toward me as if sharing a secret. "I always wake up when she leaves and opens your door."

I hold back my laughter before continuing.

"I'm so sorry, I didn't know the door made so much noise," I add hastily, nervously fidgeting with the keys in my hand. "And to be honest, I wish she didn't have to leave so early, but her day starts at dawn... We'll be more careful, I promise. And I'll check that door, maybe it needs some adjustments."

"Don't worry, young lady, I'm already used to hearing your squeaks," now I truly turn red.

He laughs seeing my expression, gives me a gentle tap with his cane as a farewell, and continues with his walk, leaving me completely dumbfounded in my doorway.

Meetings with Ghost and Melissa are becoming more frequent, at least once a week. When both have time off, we meet for dinner and catch up a bit. Sometimes at their house, other times at some restaurant in town, occasionally at our apartment. We haven't verbalized it, but thanks to our gestures, our glances, and the complicity in our daily lives, they already know it's more than official.

The last dinner we had together was a bit more special. The atmosphere seemed charged with electricity from the moment we arrived. Melissa couldn't stop smiling, and Rick seemed unable to sit still in his chair. We had barely finished the first course when she could no longer contain herself.

"I'm pregnant!" she exclaims as her husband pulls the first ultrasound of the baby they're expecting from his jacket pocket.

The black and white image passes from hand to hand. Gabriela holds it as if it were a precious, fragile object, and for a moment, I see in her gaze something I'd never noticed before: perhaps the hope of feeling something like this someday.

She's a little over three months along; they'd kept it secret since it's not the first time they've tried. They wanted to wait until it was more certain before telling anyone.

"Will you request leave?" Gabriela asks him during the conversation as we share a chocolate dessert that Melissa devours.

"The boss already knows," he responds, taking his wife's hand on the table. "Melissa has a high-risk pregnancy, she needs rest, and me being away would be constant stress. From now on, I'll stay at the base and nothing more. You'll have to find a new number two for the missions."

"That breaks my heart, friend," she says before hugging him. "But you'll be a fantastic dad, and that's all that matters now, that you're with your wife and take care of her as she deserves."

Gabriela's expression darkens for an instant, so briefly that if I weren't so attentive to each of her gestures, I would have missed it. I observe them as they embrace, feeling a mixture of joy for Rick and Melissa and, at the same time, a stab of unease that I can't identify. I know how important it is for Gabriela to have Ghost by her side. He's been her number two for the past few years, and if she has to go on a dangerous mission without him, it won't be the same.

However, what I didn't expect was for all this good streak to turn so soon. I begin to feel something is wrong when, that same evening, while preparing a special dinner, Gabriela sends me a message that makes my heart stop.

Hi! I'm on my way, but

I won't be able to stay for dinner. I'm sorry.

A long sigh escapes me as soon as I read it, and the mobile phone slips between my fingers, falling onto the kitchen counter. This means nothing other than a new mission. When she arrives home, she finds me sitting on the sofa, with tears sliding down my cheeks and a nearly overflowing glass of wine between my fingers. Her expression when she sees me is a mixture of guilt and sadness that creates a knot in my stomach.

"When?" I question, looking at her as she sits beside me and wipes the trail of moisture on my cheeks with her fingertips.

"A couple of hours," she whispers sadly. I sigh and let myself fall against her body. I know there's nothing I can do to prevent this from happening. "I'm so sorry," she whispers against my hair.

"How long will you be away?"

"I don't know, it's all classified material," she responds with that phrase I've begun to hate. Those words that open the door to uncertainty, to sleepless nights wondering if she'll be safe.

"Damn," I curse quietly.

A horrible and strange sensation takes over my entire body when I hear her speak. It's a dark thought, like a shadow that slips between us. I can't even stay still, and I get up abruptly, separating myself from her. Something tells me this mission won't be like the previous one, that something will go wrong.

"Can't you refuse this one and…?" I begin, knowing I'm asking the impossible.

"You know I can't; I have to be at the front," she responds calmly, though I know she does it, so I won't worry too much.

"Will it be safe? This time, Ghost won't be by your side, and…" the sentence escapes my mouth before I can think it through. She simply smiles and hugs me.

"It's never safe," she confesses against the skin of my neck. "But I'll do whatever it takes to come back, no matter what, even if it costs me my life."

A shiver runs from my head to my toes. Thinking she might not return freezes my blood.

"I'll come back, beautiful. I promise you," she whispers when my crying grows stronger.

The next few minutes are terrifying, at least for me. The feeling of helplessness, of being at the mercy of decisions others make, of circumstances I cannot control, completely overwhelms me.

"Here," she says suddenly, pulling slightly away from me.

I move back when her arms release me and watch as her hands go to the chain hanging from her neck. That silver chain with a small medal that she never removes, the one that has accompanied her since her first mission. The one that, according to her, has brought her luck from day one.

"What… what are you doing?" I ask when I see her take it off and put it on me.

The chain still retains the warmth of her skin when it touches mine.

"Now you have my chain, and I'll have no choice but to come back to reclaim it," she says with a smile that tries to appear carefree, but doesn't quite reflect in her gaze.

"But it's your lucky charm…" I protest, caressing the medal with my fingertips.

She hugs me from behind and leaves a soft kiss on the curve of my neck that makes me shiver.

"Now you are my lucky charm," she whispers.

Something breaks in my chest when I hear her, a mixture of love and shattering terror. I spend the last minutes by her side in her arms, with tears sliding down my cheeks, repeating like a mantra for her to be careful, to protect herself, not to take any unnecessary risks.

We remain seated on the sofa without speaking, in complete silence. I caress her face with my fingertips as if wanting to memorize every angle, every expression line before she leaves. I kiss her desperately, trying to engrave in my memory the taste of her lips or the way she sighs when I deepen the kiss.

"I need you to come back," I whisper against her mouth. "I need you whole, safe. I don't want to receive that call or that visit that wives received in war movies. I couldn't bear being told that you've..."

I can't even complete the sentence. The words get stuck in my throat.

"You won't receive calls or visits," she promises, stroking my hair. "I've survived worse things, Emma. And now I have the best reason to return. Now I have you."

She kisses me again, but this kiss is different. It's slow, as if she wanted to transmit all her determination with it, as if it were a promise that she'll return to me.

When the moment of farewell arrives, I grab her tightly, trying to keep her with me, even if just for one more minute. I cling to her jacket, her shoulders, any part of her I can reach. I have to let her go, but a part of me resists with every fiber of my being. We cry without trying to hide it. It's not easy for either of us. I know this when she releases my grip and looks at me with watery eyes and flushed cheeks.

"I love you, beautiful; don't forget it for a single day," she whispers before kissing my lips one last time and leaving my apartment.

I watch her descend the stairs without looking back. Before she can disappear, panic overwhelms me, and I run down after her, barefoot, caring about nothing more than reaching her and forcing her to hug me again.

"I love you too, Gabriela."

Seconds later, she disappears into the darkness of night, leaving an unbearable void. I'm not at ease; nothing makes me feel calm since the news of the new mission reached my ears. I just hope I'm wrong and that this bad feeling is just fear. Because I couldn't bear to lose her, much less this way, when we're just beginning to discover all that we could be together.

Chapter 14

Emma

I've spent the night wide awake. Immersed in the shadows of night, the room without her seems much emptier. Gabriela's words before leaving still circle my head: "I love you, don't forget it." They sounded more like a farewell than a promise.

The hands of the bedside clock advance with a slowness that drives me to despair. Three twenty. Four forty. Five fifteen. Bad feelings won't let me sleep. I toss and turn in the same bed I've shared so many times with her, tangling myself in sheets that still retain her scent. Her smell remains, but her warmth, her caresses, her "good night, beautiful" whispered against my hair—all that I miss. Her embraces that completely envelop me, her rhythmic breathing against my neck, the way her body molds perfectly to mine when sleeping. I need her. I need all of her.

When the sun finally floods the room with light, I decide to get up. Continuing to try to sleep won't lead to anything; I know sleep won't come. As soon as I step out of the bedroom, a feeling of heaviness settles in my chest. Something tells me today will be a hard day, harder than the previous ones, if that's possible. I drag my feet to the kitchen. The medal she left me before leaving, her lucky charm, seems to weigh a ton.

Two coffees and a rather burnt piece of toast, of course, are my breakfast before opening the bookstore. Lucille arrives first, as usual, for her first coffee of the day. As soon as she sees my face; red eyes, dark circles, paleness—she doesn't need to ask. With a simple gesture, we sit at a secluded table while I tell her everything that happened in the last few hours.

"I don't know if I can always handle this, Lucille," I confess with a long sigh, running my finger around the rim of my cup without drinking. "This uncertainty is killing me inside."

"You'll have to if you love her, Emma," she responds, taking my hands in hers and squeezing slightly to encourage me. "It's her job, her passion. And if you feel this way, it's because you're head over heels in love with her and want her close, because you want her to be safe. And each mission is a risk she takes, and you never know how it will end."

"There's a part of me that always tells me everything will be fine, but this time..." I close my eyes when that shiver I already know runs through me again, raising every hair on my body, "this time isn't the same."

I suddenly stand up and go back behind the counter, trying to keep myself busy with something. My friend comes to my side and holds my hands when they begin to shake.

"She's strong," she assures me. "She knows how to take care of herself. And she's prepared for very complicated situations. She'll return."

And although it's what I want to believe, my head and my heart don't quite accept it completely. There's something, a strange dark intuition, that refuses to disappear. And seeing Ghost enter the café doesn't make it easy for me or make me think things that aren't real. My body tenses immediately, as if sensing danger. Lucille captures the tension and uses his presence to excuse herself and go run some errands, leaving us alone.

"Has something happened?" I question quickly, going to meet him before he can approach the counter.

"No, no, relax," he puts one of his hands on my shoulder and squeezes it gently. "I just came to see how you are. Gabriela told me you were very nervous last night, devastated."

"I don't know how Melissa does it, but I... every time she's had to leave... I struggle terribly, Rick. And I can't control it. I couldn't sleep all night."

"It's completely normal," he assures me in a calm voice. "None of us feels good when we have a mission. The days drag on, the lack of communication makes it even worse... And not just for you, but for the pilots too. If I haven't gone this time it's because Melissa is going to give me the best gift of my life and I don't want to cause her any kind of stress that could worsen her condition. But I would have gone, because even at the risk of losing everything, it's what I love doing most... and I've been on so many missions with Gabriela that I hate leaving her alone."

"I know... I don't know if it's because of the time you've been working together, but you two are like copies of each other," I add, making him laugh.

"Gabriela is like my sister, almost from the first moment we met. Sometimes she closes up a lot, or doesn't share too much about her life, but she knows she'll always have me here, no matter what."

"She does know that, I assure you," I sigh.

I serve him a coffee and give him something sweet to go with it and, taking advantage of the quiet hours, we sit at one of the tables near the window to chat.

"Her strength is… indisputable, Emma. I think I've never known anyone like her. The dedication and passion she has for her work surpasses anyone's, that's why she's become the best. Many thought the squadron wouldn't function with her as the leader, they literally said that a female boss would ruin it. And they've all eaten their words because, thanks to her, the entire team has strengthened and improved like never before," I smile proudly at what he tells me. "Sometimes, she's even given some of them a slap on the head, they would brag about situations, make tasteless jokes… And Gabriela has handled all of them in a matter of minutes. In fact, if my count is right, it's been a long time since any of them has said anything like that, not even behind her back—they fear and respect her," we laugh, knowing what she's capable of when she sets her mind to it.

The conversation flows naturally as the café begins to fill with the first regular customers. Rick tells me anecdotes from recent years: Gabriela's difficult beginnings as squadron leader, complicated missions, hard training sessions, how they both have overcome obstacles together, and how, no matter what happened, they've always supported each other during missions.

"However, even though I've known her for many years, I've never seen her so happy. Since she met you..." he pauses thoughtfully, trying to find the right words. "She's a different Gabriela. At work she's the same," he clarifies, "but as a person... she's brighter. She smiles, she opens up much more, know what I mean?"

"Yes," I answer with a smile.

"You make her better, if that's possible. The light she had lost has returned. I don't know what the future holds for you, I hope good things, very good things, because you're made for each other. I see in you two the same thing I see in Melissa and me. We made ours work, even being apart for a while. And if we could, with many complications, you two can too. You just have to remember that the relationship is something between two people, just yours, and therefore, it's your joint decisions that will help you move forward or not. And, from the little I've seen, something tells me it will be that way forever."

His words calm me. I already knew I'm with one of the strongest women I could have found, but everything I've discovered about her today makes me feel more at ease.

However, this feeling of peace, although somewhat sad due to her absence, doesn't last long. The next day, in the afternoon, when the café was busiest, Rick visits us again. His contorted expression and nervous gaze doesn't bode well for me.

Lucille, who is helping me with orders, sees him before I do. Our gazes meet for an instant, and I know she has caught the same thing I have: something is terribly wrong. Without a word, she takes the tray from my hands and relieves me, leaving me free to go out and talk to him.

"Emma…" he sighs as soon as I approach, and his voice sounds very different. There's a tension in it that I've never heard before.

"What? What happened?" I ask frantically as soon as I step onto the sidewalk.

"I'm sorry, I..." he stammers, running a hand through his hair in a clear gesture of desperation.

"Spit it out, Ghost, for God's sake!" I shout, grabbing him by the shirt and shaking him, about to explode.

"There's… there's been an incident on the mission."

"What?" My grip weakens, but I don't let go. I know if I do, I'll fall.

"We don't know much yet, the conditions aren't clear, but what we do know is that Gabriela's plane was hit."

The world around me seems to stop. The sounds of the street fade as if someone had suddenly turned down the volume. I only hear the beat of my own heart hammering against my temple.

"How badly hit?" I sigh.

Rick swallows, his eyes avoiding mine for a second that seems like an eternity.

"I don't know," he admits. "My boss said her plane had been shot down. They don't know the damage it could have caused, not even if… if she's still alive. Damn, I should have gone with her. I should have flown by her side," he repeats, clenching his fists and turning his gaze to the sky.

Gabriela hit, plane shot down. A flood of images crosses my mind at that moment. Gabriela in the cockpit, lights flashing, alarms sounding, an explosion, metal twisting, flames, smoke… and then nothing. Emptiness. Nothingness. I step away from Ghost, trying to keep standing, but everything spins. The facades of buildings tilt, the ground seems to undulate beneath my feet. My vision narrows, as if I were looking through a tunnel.

"She's dead… Gabriela is dead," I whisper, feeling myself slowly suffocate.

The air fails me. Panic takes over, making me gasp for oxygen that seems to have disappeared from the atmosphere; I know I'm about to faint. Everything turns black. I can feel each beat of my heart like a blow against my ribs. Cold sweat runs down my back, soaking my blouse. My hands shake uncontrollably.

"It can't be, it can't be," I repeat, though I'm not sure if the words leave my mouth or just resonate in my head. "She promised me she would come back… she promised me…"

I squeeze the charm as if that could bring her back to me.

"Emma, Emma!" I hear my name from afar, muffled, as if it came from the other side of a very thick glass.

But it's too late. The pressure overwhelms me, and my body, this time, won't deal with it. The last thing I feel before darkness completely engulfs me is the cold of the pavement against my cheek and the certainty that half of my soul has just been brutally torn away.

Chapter 15

Gabriela

The impact arrives without warning.

One instant I'm executing an evasion maneuver, and the next, the world explodes around me. The roar of the explosion deafens me, so intense that for several seconds I hear nothing but a high-pitched ringing inside my skull.

The control panel goes crazy, and my plane now resembles a wounded animal that shakes and convulses, resisting any attempt at control on my part. Through the cockpit glass, I watch as fragments of the right wing break off, torn away by air pressure and explosion damage.

The plane begins to spin out of control. It bears no resemblance to the precise, calculated turn of an evasive maneuver; it's more like the chaotic movement of an object that has lost its aerodynamics. The G-force pushes me against the seat with such intensity that, for a moment, I fear my ribs will give way under the pressure. It feels as if someone placed a heavy slab on my chest and keeps pushing it with increasing force.

Again and again, with each spin, earth and sky exchange positions and disorient me. The horizon is no longer a straight line, but a curve that twists and contorts as if the entire universe has gone mad.

The hydraulic systems begin to fail, emitting a high-pitched moan that I feel more than hear, as if the plane screams in pain. The controls don't respond. There's no exit, no solution, no way to regain control of 22 tons of military technology plummeting toward the ground at nearly 200 miles per hour.

And then I remember Emma. Her face appears with astonishing clarity: the tiny wrinkles around her eyes when she smiles, the way a strand of hair always falls across her forehead, no matter how many times she pushes it away, her fingers interlaced with mine. The promise I made to return. The charm I left hanging from her neck. The life we've barely begun to build together.

I reach for the ejection handle, aware that abandoning the plane means surrendering to the unknown, but remaining in it means embracing certain death.

In the last second before activating the system, while my fighter continues its deadly spiral toward the ground, I register one final thought: "Emma, I'll come back to you. I promised."

And then I pull the handle.

A controlled explosion catapults me upward with overwhelming force. The temperature changes immediately, and rotation begins. The ejection seat doesn't rise in a straight line; it spins erratically on its axis. The world becomes a carousel where sky and earth alternate so quickly that my brain can't process the images. I see only fragments: the blue of the sky, the ochre of the desert, the black smoke my plane leaves as it falls.

For an instant, I hang suspended at the highest point of the trajectory, at that point where the launch inertia balances with gravity. It's a moment of impossible calm. I float weightlessly in a limbo between heaven and earth.

And then, I fall.

The parachute opens with a sound like a giant sheet being shaken by the wind. The sudden deceleration makes the harness dig into my shoulders and crotch with such force that, for a moment, I believe it's broken my collarbones. It's a sharp, focused pain. And then, silence as I descend slowly over the desert.

The mission changes radically. It's no longer about completing a strategic objective. Now it's much simpler yet infinitely more complex: survive.

Luckily, before touching ground, I observe my plane crash with a massive explosion. There's no need to approach it to activate the self-destruction of critical equipment that could fall into enemy hands.

I reach the ground in minutes, my legs giving way under my weight upon touching earth. I hurriedly free myself from the harnesses and move away from the plane, walking toward a rock formation. For a moment, I consider activating an emergency beacon to indicate my position, but I prefer not to be detected by the enemy. My right shoulder throbs with sharp pain; it's probably dislocated. My entire body is a map of bruises and cuts, some superficial, others deep enough to leave permanent scars.

If I survive to see them.

I tear a piece of my pants and use it as an impro-vised sling, immobilizing my arm against my chest. It hurts, but at least it will prevent the damage from worsening.

I lean against one of the rocks, seeking minimal shade, and evaluate the situation. How does one survive in the desert without a single drop of water? The answer is as simple as it is terrifying: you can't. No matter how well trained I am, no matter how many extreme situations I've overcome, there are limits the human body simply cannot surpass.

Pain runs from head to toe, every movement agonizing. The sun presses down with increasing intensity. I try to rest, though the word "rest" almost seems a euphemism for what I truly fear: dying here, alone, under this scorching sun. Indifferent. It's not death itself I fear, but what will happen afterward. Emma waiting for a call from me that will never come. Emma receiving a visit from some army officer or perhaps Ghost to give her the news of my death. Emma collapsing upon learning I didn't keep my promise to return.

I try to stay awake with memories of her. The moments we spent together, her laughter, our plans for the future. For a moment, I manage to smile. Everything seems so distant now...

Dehydration begins to take a more evident toll. My vision blurs, the contours of the rocks become hazy. And when I have my first hallucination, I know I'm going to die.

A boy riding a white dromedary. He's no more than twelve years old, his skin bronzed and dressed in Bedouin style. I could at least leave this world believing I'm with Emma and not with a non-existent boy and dromedary.

"Hello, are you okay?" he asks, commanding the dromedary to kneel so he can dismount and approach me.

"My plane has crashed," I explain.

For an instant, I consider not responding. I know it's a hallucination, but I prefer to die believing I'm accompanied rather than in silence.

"You better drink something," he indicates, handing me a canteen that seems too real.

"What's your name, and why do you speak my language perfectly?"

"Better drink," he insists.

I simply shrug and play along. I accept the drink, even knowing it's not real, though for a hallucination, the liquid inside the goatskin canteen certainly seems real.

"What is it?" I ask, feeling better almost immediately.

"Laban rayeb; fermented milk. It's good for traveling through the desert."

"Will you tell me your name?"

"Amir Iverson. You better come with me. You won't survive if you stay here."

"You know in my country, there's a famous actress with the same last name as yours?" I joke while trying to stand up.

"She's my mother," the kid responds naturally.

I shake my head, and a smile escapes me. At least my hallucination has a sense of humor.

"Come with me," the boy insists. "My village is near here. Jadir will carry us both. He's the fastest dromedary in the area. They'll help you there."

I decide to trust him, not because I believe he's real, but because I have nothing to lose riding a white dromedary, following a mirage to an imaginary village. If

I'm going to die, let it be chasing one last hope, however false it may be.

"Hold on as tight as you can, we'll arrive soon."

We cross the desert faster than I could ever imagine, and upon reaching the village, people stop to look at us with curiosity. I feel weak, like I might faint at any moment. However, the boy shouts and gives orders in a language I don't understand. Within seconds, two women—practically carbon copies of each other with thirty years' difference—who I imagine are his mother and grandmother, accompanied by more people, come out to help me.

"Who is this woman?"

"I don't know, she just told me her plane had been shot down," responds the boy as an older woman kneels to examine my arm.

"Gabriela, my name is Gabriela. Your grandson saved my life," I tell her as they carry me into the house. "Is all this real?"

"Yes, don't worry, you're safe. My name is Istar. What happened?" asks the younger woman, with beautiful dark eyes.

"My plane was hit. I need a phone to let people know I'm still alive."

"First, we need to relocate that shoulder and treat your wounds."

"Relocate…? Oh, God!!" I don't have time to think when the woman sets it, causing the pain to diminish and confirming this isn't a hallucination.

Minutes later, while she finishes treating my wounds, and they give me something to eat, the boy returns, sitting beside me.

"Thank you, Amir, you saved my life," I thank him, seeing the pride in his mother's eyes. "You know Victoria Iverson is blonde, and your mother is brunette, right?" I tease, though I only succeed in making them both burst into laughter.

"She's my other mother," responds the boy, dying of laughter.

"Yes. Victoria and I met during one of her movie shoots. We fell in love and haven't separated since, except when she travels for work, like now."

I listen attentively to the story she tells me and decide to share mine.

"She must be very worried now," the woman sighs. "Don't worry, we'll contact the American embassy, and soon you'll be with her."

Chapter 16

Emma

Two days have passed without any news from Ghost. I've sent him dozens of messages, but he always responds the same way. A terse: "I still don't know anything; I'll let you know." And that doesn't sit well with me. Since the moment I fainted, the Literary Café has closed its doors, forced by my doctor and by Lucille, who has even slept at my place to take care of me and prevent me from doing anything crazy.

She sets our first coffee of the day on the living room table. She knows I'm not going to eat anything, and for once, she doesn't offer or force me to do so.

"Were you able to get any rest?" I pick up the coffee and take a small sip. I keep the cup in my hands to warm them.

"The pills do their job," I respond with my gaze fixed on some indeterminate point. "But I haven't stopped dreaming about Gabriela."

Always the same dream: her plane crashing in flames against an endless desert. I always wake up just before impact, with a dry throat and sheets soaked in sweat.

"I don't understand why they're not telling you anything."

"Either they don't know anything, or if they do, it's very bad. I'm starting to lose what little hope I have," I admit, letting tears roll down my cheeks.

"Never that, Emma," she says, before hugging me. "We know Gabriela is very strong, one of the best in her field."

The coffee cools between my hands as I shake my head.

"But if she's been hit, it doesn't matter, Lucille, it doesn't matter at all."

"We don't know that," she insists, brushing a strand of hair from my face. "She's trained to overcome dangerous and difficult situations; who's to say this isn't one of those times?"

I'm about to continue denying it, but just at that moment, the doorbell rings. We exchange a quick glance, and I jump up to open the door. My eyes widen in surprise when I see it's Melissa.

"Where's your husband?" I ask her before she can say anything.

"He sent me for you, Emma. They've found Gabriela. They're taking her to the military hospital. Rick has already left for there."

"Do you know how she is?" I sigh, bringing my hands to my chest.

"No, I only know we need to go to the base hospital. They landed a few minutes ago, and they're attending to her."

Without wasting time, the three of us rush out of my apartment. I don't even realize I'm wearing slippers until I get in the car. Melissa drives and takes us to the hospital without saying a single word. At the door itself, Ghost waits for us. His face is serious but calm. He strokes his beard as we approach.

"Where is she? How is she?" I question as soon as I see him, trying to look behind him. Several colleagues stand a few steps back, also waiting.

"The doctors are attending to her right now. They'll tell us something soon, and we'll go in as soon as they allow us," he explains, so I won't insist on entering. "Can you believe she's alive thanks to a kid?"

"What?" Melissa, Lucille, and I are left open-mouthed hearing this.

With a tired smile, Ghost relates what happened. He describes how Gabriela, dehydrated and about to die under the desert sun, thought she was hallucinating when a boy dressed in Bedouin style and riding a white dromedary approached her and spoke to her in perfect English. He nearly has a fit of laughter recounting that the boy was the son of Victoria Iverson, the Hollywood actress we all know, who was spending a few days vacationing with his Bedouin grandmother. She's had a lot of luck, perhaps too much, but I won't be the one to complain. Gabriela is alive. She's here.

The hospital's automatic doors open, and several doctors come out discussing something in low voices. Seeing us, they stop their conversation and head directly toward Ghost.

"Major Díaz is stable. They treated her wounds well where they picked her up. She'll need to rest for a few weeks until she's recovered. She can't make any physical efforts until her shoulder heals and the wounds heal.

Watch her closely, she's a bit stubborn and intends to walk out of the hospital today."

"Don't worry about that, doctor," I interject, with a smile as I dry the tears of relief rolling down my cheeks. "I'll take care of that."

They allow us to enter, and the hallway seems endless until we reach her room. When the door opens, our eyes meet. Her eyes, though tired, shine with an intensity that takes my breath away. She's thinner, with a bulky bandage on her shoulder and small burns and bruises visible on her arms, but she's alive. Alive and smiling at seeing me. I cross the room in three strides and lean down to hug her with all the care I can. I don't want to hurt her more than she already is.

"I was so worried about you…" I whisper against her neck as she tightens the embrace, ignoring the pain. "Are you… are you okay?" I ask, taking her face in my hands, my thumbs caressing her sunburned cheeks.

"Right now, better than ever," she murmurs and, not caring who might be watching, brings her lips to mine in a kiss that conveys everything words cannot express. As we part, her eyes show concern. "They told me you fainted."

I smile, remembering the terrible moment when they announced her plane had been shot down.

"Thinking you might have died made me lose consciousness from the stress itself," I confess, intertwining my fingers with hers. "But I'm fine, I've been at home for a couple of days, resting. I thought I'd never see you again, and..."

"Shh, it's okay, that didn't happen. Your memory kept me awake long enough until they found me. If these gentlemen let me, we'll be home soon," she says more seriously, looking at the doctors.

Both Ghost and I hold back our laughter; she's not going to make it easy for the doctor, and he knows it well.

"You should stay in the hospital," the doctor begins, running a hand through his gray hair. "However, I see you'll be well cared for if I let you go home, though, in any case, that will be tomorrow," he raises a finger, seeing Gabriela's victorious smile. "You'll spend tonight here. And only if they assure me you won't make physical efforts or do anything that endangers your condition."

"Don't worry, doctor," Rick then adds, positioning himself on the other side. "If necessary, we'll tie her to the headboard so she doesn't move."

"Maybe I'd like that more than you might think…" Gabriela whispers with a wink, quietly enough that only Ghost and I hear her, causing me to slap her leg while I turn red looking at her friend, who laughs and rolls his eyes.

Colleagues and superiors come to see her throughout the day. They notice my presence and, contrary to what I expected, thank me for being by her side and caring for her as I do. They're proud of the woman before me and all she's accomplished, as well as how brave she's been after what happened.

When night falls, we're left alone. She makes room for me in the bed, and we hug again for the next few minutes. Even the silence is pleasant in her arms.

"I thought I would die in the desert," she begins to relate, catching my attention. I sit up and observe the tears on her face. All that fear she's been holding back is now coming out, "if it hadn't been for Amir and his eagerness to travel the desert with his dromedary…"

"But you were very lucky, you're alive, and home, safe and sound," I whisper, cleaning the moisture from her cheeks.

"I almost lost the rest of the squadron…"

"You were very brave, love, extremely so," I caress her jaw with my fingertips. "You almost gave your life for it, and you see they'll always be grateful to you. They're alive, you too, and that's the most important thing now."

"But what if next time it's not like that? I have many doubts, Emma."

"Doubts?"

"Flying fighter jets has always been my dream," she confesses, looking at the ceiling. "But the fear I felt this time…" she pauses, swallowing. "And the worst part is that I wasn't afraid for my life. My greatest fear was never seeing you again."

Her words make me cry, surprised by what she's confessing to me.

"I don't know if I'll fly again," she adds almost in a whisper.

"You're going to leave your career?"

"I don't want to not come home; I don't want to spend more nights in a hospital with these pains," her fingers intertwine with mine. "I want our life, to be with you, and nothing more."

She tries to sit up, but I gently stop her and lie down again at her side, hugging her carefully so as not to hurt her.

"I want all that too," I add before kissing her, "but I can't let you abandon your career. I think right now you're speaking out of fear because of everything that's happened, and I know that when you say something, you're very clear about it. But truly, with all that it entails, I want you to wait until you're recovered to make such an important decision. You'll have a few weeks of recovery, and when this is over, everything will be clear."

"And if I finally decide to quit?"

"I'll be here to support you. Just as I would if you decide to continue."

"Are you sure about that?"

"Very sure, like never before."

"But you've suffered so much, beautiful."

"I know, and it will hurt to have to separate from you for other missions," I admit, smiling despite the tears. "However, you're happy flying, and I'm not going to let what makes you happiest in this life disappear."

She smiles before speaking.

"What makes me happiest right now is you, Emma. Maybe it's time to stop and take new paths," she says, taking my hands.

"Maybe, but don't make decisions lightly, okay?"

"Okay..."

This time it's me who cradles her in my arms, enjoying the miracle of having her back. Her breathing becomes deeper and more regular as she surrenders to exhaustion. She must have gone through a lot to be thinking about leaving her dream. Deep in my heart, a part of me is happy about it; I wouldn't like to go through another hell like this in the future. However, I feel guilty and selfish for thinking that way. Flying is her life, and I don't want this decision to affect her in the future. Alt hough the scale weighs more to one side than the other, I'm glad she's going to think about it over the coming weeks.

Chapter 17

Gabriela

Days crawl past my eyes with unbearable slowness, each one harder than the last. Recovery weighs on my back, proving far slower than I imagined. It drains my patience completely. Pain chases me with every movement, no matter how small, and that frustrates me. Even the simple gesture of reaching for a glass of water triggers lightning bolts that shoot from my shoulder to my fingertips.

My whole life is action, speed, adrenaline. Making decisions in tenths of a second. Having to stay calm and lying down for so many hours is killing me. It's a kind of cruel torture. I can't adapt, no matter how easy Emma and the rest of the squadron members make it for me. Being part of the military elite means constant motion, and I feel I won't get used to a quieter life. I'm starting to become convinced of it.

After fifteen days confined at home, the entire squadron visits me. They enter like a gust of energy, filling the apartment with laughter and the aroma of homemade food that Reaper has brought. For a moment, the atmosphere changes completely, and I let myself get carried away by the normalcy, even if it's temporary.

"Night Hawk! You should see the new flight patterns we're practicing," Ghost comments while devouring a sandwich. "The Colonel has implemented some of your tactical suggestions."

Bulldog nods enthusiastically beside him before taking a swig of his beer.

"Your evasion maneuver from the last combat is being included in the training manual. You're becoming a legend even from the couch," he jokes.

Emma notices my desperation when my colleagues leave and my smile disappears.

"What's wrong?" she questions, sitting beside me.

"I want to fly again," I blurt out with a sigh of frustration.

"I know. And very soon you'll be able to."

"Soon? I've been stuck here for two weeks, and I'm climbing the walls. I want to get out now," I add, frustrated and angry.

"Until the doctor clears you, that won't happen, Gabriela," she responds seriously. "If you'd like, we can take a walk to the base, visit Melissa and Rick, but nothing more."

"I'm sick of taking walks, damn it!"

The words explode with more force than I intended. It's not the first time this week my temper has overflowed this way, and I know it's not right. The hours in this house are beginning to weigh on me too much. But things are starting to spiral out of control inside me, and I don't know how to stop them. I try to sit up, and since I can't do it by myself, she helps me.

"I know it's difficult."

"No, you don't know, Emma!" I interrupt her harshly, before she can continue speaking. "Right now I feel like an idiot. A complete burden. I can't even stand up by myself, for God's sake!"

"You're not a burden, Gabriela, you have never been. You're not used to this routine, and I understand that because I see it in your eyes and in your gestures every day. But you would never be a burden to me."

"No? You're having to leave your work in Lucille's hands."

"She does it gladly, and I'm grateful to her because that way I can spend more time with you."

"And is it worth it having to put up with me like this?"

I watch her, her expression turning serious again. She massages her temples and sighs before moving closer.

"Being able to take care of you and enjoy your company almost twenty-four hours a day is all I want to do, Gabriela. I don't mind spending fewer hours at the café. My business will always be there, and my friend loves working in it, so it's not a problem. I know the situation isn't easy, but all I want is to make the most of our time together until you fully recover. I know that when that happens, you'll go back to flying, and new missions will keep us apart again. So yes, it's worth it to me. You can yell at me all you want; I know it's the pain that's really doing it, not you. But that won't make me leave or stop caring for you. Did you hear me?"

I don't respond, anger still coursing through my gut.

"I'm here because I want to be," she insists when she sees I say nothing.

"Sometimes I don't think it seems that way," the words escape me without thinking, surprising her.

"Do you really think I'm doing this out of obligation?" she asks back, angry.

"What I think is that you don't know what you're getting into. This is crap, Emma. Just a pause. As soon as I can fly again, they'll send me to another base, almost certainly another country. Because that's how this really is. One day, I'm here, and another day, I'm not. I'm not someone who stays."

"What the hell does that mean, Gabriela?" She's hurt, I know, but it's reality, and she needs to know it.

"It means there probably won't be an 'us' in the long term."

The woman in front of me goes still, static. She's processing what I just said. The silence starts to weigh, becoming increasingly tense. I look away, a little regretful about what I just blurted out. But deep down, it's what I think, though it doesn't mean it's what I want.

"Are you saying it's over?" her voice trembles; I know she's holding back tears.

"All I want is to avoid breaking you," I respond, biting my lower lip painfully. "I know I'll end up hurting you like everyone else. And I love you too much to do that."

"I didn't know you felt that way," she murmurs, shifting her gaze to the window so I won't see the suffering in her eyes. "I thought you were committed to our relationship."

"I just want to be realistic, Emma," I insist, though each of my words feels like flesh being torn from bone. "I've always lived like this. Base after base, country after country. That's how it is."

"So what am I to you? Just a pastime?" This time, her tears overflow, and she spits the words with rage.

"No, you're everything I ever wanted in my life. But I'm afraid I'll hurt you when I have to leave."

"What if you don't have to leave? What if that changes?"

"I don't know how… I don't know how to stay still. I don't know how to depend on someone. To feel useless."

"You're not useless, Gabriela. You're hurt, but you're also healing. All you want is to pilot a life you're currently unable to control. But I'm here with you, for better or worse. Look… if you decide to leave someday, I'll understand. But don't push me away when what I really want is to stay."

We look at each other in silence. I turn my gaze away from hers, unable to hold it.

"I don't want to hurt you," I repeat, not knowing what else to say.

"Then don't."

Chapter 18

Gabriela

A Few Weeks Later

"Major Díaz, I don't know how you've managed it, but you've recovered in record time." The doctor's words make me smile as he reviews the latest X-rays.

It hasn't been easy at all. I've had to overcome many moments of frustration, and the pain sometimes became unbearable.

"I could recommend a calm, gradual return to work," he continues, lowering the X-rays and looking at me over his glasses with resignation, "but I'm sure you won't pay the slightest attention to me."

"I assure you I'm in condition to resume at one hundred percent," I respond immediately. "I wouldn't put the rest of the squadron in danger because of me for a moment."

"And I respect that," he adds, extending his hand to conclude our final session. "Any abnormality or strange sensation, don't hesitate to return, agreed?"

I assure him I will and leave the hospital with a smile that fades as soon as I remember Emma. Since the last time we argued, the relationship hasn't been the same. I'd love to run from the base to her café and tell her the good news, but given the situation, I don't. It's been a few days since we've seen each other; the little we've talked has been to let her know I was about to be cleared. And it hurts. It hurts to see how we had everything and how, because of my fears and everything the medical leave caused me, it's broken.

I walk the path to the residential area of the base from memory, my feet automatically taking me to Rick and Melissa's house. If there's anyone who can help me clear my thoughts, it's them. Plus, Melissa is about to give birth, and the idea of new life amid so much uncertainty feels very comforting.

With just one look when he opens the door, Ghost knows I've been cleared.

"I knew it!" he exclaims, giving me a strong pat on the back. "Nobody keeps Night Hawk grounded for long."

Melissa rests on the sofa, surrounded by pillows and blankets. Her belly, enormous at thirty-nine weeks.

"How are you doing, Mel?"

"Extremely fat," she jokes, caressing her belly and making us smile. "But good, in the last few hours I've felt some contractions, so the moment is approaching."

The joy in her voice is contagious. For a few minutes, they tell me how the baby seems to be playing soccer inside the womb, how the gynecologist has warned them to be ready to rush to the hospital at any moment.

Seeing the papers in my hand, she can't help but ask:

"Have you told Emma yet?"

"No... We haven't spoken for a couple of days," I confess, letting out a sigh I didn't even know I was holding.

"What a pair of stubborn heads," Melissa blurts out, sitting up with some difficulty. "I really don't understand you two! You love each other, and instead of fighting for your relationship, you've abandoned it."

"Honey, you shouldn't…" Ghost tries to mediate, but his wife is right.

"No, deep down, what she says is true," I interrupt. "I behaved like a complete idiot. But I didn't tell her anything that wasn't true. My life has been based on traveling from base to base. And my time at this one is running out. Soon they'll station us elsewhere."

"You don't know that yet," he replies.

"Yes, yes, I do," I respond, lowering my gaze. "Two days ago, during one of my last training sessions with the physical therapist, the Colonel stopped by to say hello."

"Well…"

"What?" Melissa questions. "He wanted to check on your recovery, right?"

"The Colonel doesn't make courtesy visits," her husband clarifies.

"That's right," I affirm. "Just as he came by here a few days ago offering you a permanent position here… He came by there to let me know he had something important to discuss with me, but that he would do it once I was cleared."

"That's why you haven't gone to see Emma, right?" my friend asks.

"What am I going to tell her? I've been cleared, but I'm leaving soon? If there's anything left between us, it will destroy it, and I don't know if I can bear it."

Melissa sits beside me, gently caressing my back, knowing I'm not doing well.

"It's not easy, Gabriela. But you love her, and she loves you, and at minimum she deserves to know: one, that you're okay, and two, that you're going to leave."

And, as usual, I can't ignore reality. She's right, I have to do it, but first I want to have full confirmation and the details.

Emma

Customers stream in and out without pause. Any other time, I'd feel overwhelmed or wish for less traffic so I could rest. Right now, though, I'm grateful they don't leave me a single second to think. Because every time I do, she occupies every one of my thoughts. Has she been cleared? Is she okay? Does she have the same pain in her chest that I do?

As if she heard me, she appears at the café late in the afternoon. It's been several days since we've seen each other, and, although things aren't good between us, I'm thankful to have her in front of me.

"Sorry for the wait," I apologize, lowering my voice and approaching her as soon as I finish attending to a couple of curious browsers.

"Don't worry... Do you think we can talk when your shift ends?"

"Uh, yes, sure." I glance at the clock on the wall, just over half an hour left before closing. "If you're not in a hurry... in a few minutes I'll close, and then we can talk more privately."

"Great."

Gabriela sits on one of the bar stools to look at her phone. I observe her discreetly while attending to the last customers. Her gaze remains concentrated on the screen, but her fingers drum nervously on the counter. She's serious; it's clear the conversation she wants to have will mark us, and something tells me it will be one of the last, if not the last.

Little by little, I start to clean up and put things away, letting the customers know it's time to leave. It's somewhat earlier than usual, but nobody says anything, and I have crucial reasons for doing it. Once the café is closed, and without saying a word, we go upstairs to my place.

"Would you like something to drink or eat?" I ask as soon as I close the door.

"No need, thanks. I don't have much appetite," she indicates with a gesture of her hand.

"Well, what do you want to talk about?"

We sit facing each other at the kitchen island. I think she notices the fear in my words. She places her hands on the countertop and sighs before speaking.

"I'm leaving for the United States," she says bluntly.

Her words fall like a burning nail. But I'm not surprised; I knew this was going to happen.

"How long have you known?"

"It became official this morning."

"When do you…?" I try not to cry, but the pain overwhelms me and tears overflow my eyes. I can't even finish the sentence.

"At dawn."

"Damn," I sigh.

I get up abruptly and go to my bedroom. I need space, air, or something to relieve this pressure in my chest that threatens to suffocate me. The feeling running through me at this moment is indescribable. Everything I've been holding back since that argument begins to sink me.

I stifle the sobbing in my throat, but I stop doing so when her arms surround me. In that instant, I let all the pain out. She holds me, though we end up on the floor, hugging, crying. The "us" is over, and there's no turning back.

Chapter 19

Emma

Her fingers trace my bare back with the slowness of someone who knows she's touching something for the last time. She pauses at my nape, leaving a sweet kiss that sounds like goodbye. Her body presses against mine. Too painful. Maybe we shouldn't have done this; maybe the farewell should have been different, but this is our language, and only we need to understand it.

We've loved each other one last time. Without words. And now we're tangled, with sweat still running down our skin, with breathing interrupted by the mixture of desire and tears that we both suppress, knowing what will happen next. Her body pulls away from mine; she knows all too well that staying longer will only be worse for both of us. I turn and lean on my left arm, watching her dress in the moonlight.

"I never wanted you to leave," I tell her, releasing a long sigh that sounds like surrender. It's a confession she already knew.

"I know."

She kneels on the bed, moving closer to me again.

She kisses me with fear, perhaps with guilt. It's our way of saying goodbye. When she pulls away and our eyes meet, words flow from my mouth without measure. Not with harm, but with truth and pain.

"Don't write to me," I ask in a whisper.

"I won't," she says with a sigh.

"Not because I don't want to hear from you. I always will. But because I couldn't keep living."

She nods. She understands. It's painful to get news from someone you can't have and will never see again.

She stands up, averting her gaze to avoid meeting mine. Each step costs more than the one before. I know it. She finishes dressing in silence and begins her departure. Before leaving the room, she turns and takes something from her pocket. She approaches and leaves it in my hands before leaving, but I can't look at it, my eyes fixed on her. I continue watching her, now crying. This image will be etched in our memory for the rest of our lives.

When the apartment door closes, the end becomes much more real. And the truth is, I don't even know if I want to continue living in this present. It's then that I look at the object, a small wolf carved in wood with an inscription: "It will always protect you." Now I really don't know how I'm going to survive.

A few hours later

I pour coffee and serve people automatically. I don't even think about whether I'm doing it right; in fact, I don't even care what people might think at this precise moment. I return to reality when Lucille snaps her fingers in front of my eyes.

"What's wrong with you? I thought I was talking to you until I realized you weren't listening," she protests.

"Gabriela left last night."

"She left? Where to?"

"To the United States," I respond with a huff.

"What? Why?"

"She was cleared a couple of days ago. Within hours, she met with her superiors, and they promoted her and even decorated her for what happened in the last mission. Now she has more responsibilities and, there-fore, can't stay here."

"And she told you all this…"

"A few hours before leaving. She came here, we went upstairs, and she laid it all out," I admit, trying not to start crying again.

"And she left, just like that?" she insists, con-fused.

"We slept together," I confess, lowering my gaze. "It was our goodbye."

"Damn, Emma… You'll at least stay in touch; what you have can't end like this."

"No, that won't happen. Knowing about her and not being able to have her would be much harder. And yes, it's obvious that what we had is over. The last few weeks have been a real mess, and everything we had van-ished," I acknowledge, biting my lower lip painfully.

"But..."

"No buts, Luci, it's over, and that's it. I don't want to keep talking about this, please."

I come out from behind the counter and hide in the stockroom. Tears run down my cheeks again, and I don't want either the customers or her to see me like this. Minutes later, the bell rings, announcing the entrance of a new customer, and I go out to attend to them. But to my surprise, I find myself face to face with Melissa. From her face, I'm sure she's about to give birth.

"What are you doing here? Shouldn't you be resting at home?" I ask as soon as I see her.

"I needed some fresh air between contractions," I smile, knowing the countdown has begun. "And I wanted to know how you're doing after Gabriela left."

I take a breath and release it slowly before answering.

"I'm not good, you know that," she nods slowly, leaning on the counter. "I don't... I don't even know how to feel, honestly. One day, we were betting on our relationship, making future plans, and the next she's on her way to the United States. I don't know, Mel, I thought what we had would work, but the accident."

"The accident brought out the worst in Gabriela, and she didn't know how to handle it. She's had a hard time, and the trauma and everything that happened was too much for her. But that's no excuse either. I told her that before she left, and she couldn't even argue with me."

"I know she never wanted to hurt me. I'm completely sure she loves me. But what she said, the way and manner she did it, how she distanced herself from me giving up… I couldn't row alone. Now it's over," I admit, shrugging.

"You shouldn't have had to do it alone, Emma. A relationship involves two people," I nod. I think the same. "She didn't leave very convinced, I can assure you that. I think she acted more out of not knowing how to handle the whole situation than for wanting that promotion."

"I know…"

"She told us she'd been with you."

"Yes…"

"And I thought I'd have you both as babysitters for my precious daughter," she adds jokingly to make me smile.

"Well, you'll have me here when you need me; you already know that," I assure her, gently caressing her left arm. "And her, even from far away, I think she'll also make sure the little one is well cared for and doesn't lack anything."

She nods and smiles, instinctively looking toward her belly. She allows me to vent for a few minutes, but I reach the same conclusion as with Lucille. Nothing was going to change. Gabriela has gone more than 4,300 miles away from me, and nothing or no one can undo that, no matter how much it hurts.

Chapter 20

Gabriela

A Week Later

The new job and the team surrounding me have completely exceeded my expectations. The opportunity they've given me is perfect, and, at least for a few hours, they make me feel a little better. Yet, though I'm happy to be back in my country, my apartment, and what has been my home, I have a choking sensation in my chest that I can't shake.

I miss Emma more each day. Never in my life have I felt something so intense for another woman. With my work, I've barely had lasting relationships; I don't think any have been; nobody wanted to stay despite everything. Except her.

"And now that you've found her, you go and mess it up. You're an idiot, Gabriela!" I mutter to myself, kicking one of the many cardboard boxes I still haven't unpacked.

A couple of knocks on the door bring me back to reality and make me set aside my frustration. By the sound, I know it's Mr. Kreen, my lifelong neighbor. An old USAF veteran with whom I've been able to unburden myself since I was old enough to remember. He always understood the demands of my job and has always been there to help me when I needed it most.

"Kicking the boxes again?" he asks, raising his bushy eyebrows. His aged voice makes me smile.

"You know me too well, Bill."

"What's wrong?" he inquires, sitting on the sofa.

"What's wrong is that I'm an idiot, I've let my fears and insecurities destroy my life," I confess, letting out a snort of frustration while massaging my temples.

"Don't you think you're exaggerating a little, child?" I slowly shake my head. "Is there something you haven't told me about your stop in Atrivia?" I sigh and nod. With a gentle gesture, he pats the sofa with his palm and asks me to sit beside him.

"I left the love of my life there," I admit, feeling tears begin to well in my eyes.

"You met someone and you left her for work?" he questions, surprised.

I nod and tell him in detail what happened during my stay in Zelenova. I tell him about Emma, her café, how we gradually fell in love and began our life together. How we thought we were made for each other. And, of course, I also mention how the accident broke everything. Well, I broke it, the accident was just an excuse.

"You're in love, Gabriela. And you're afraid because it's the first time in your life you've felt something so intense," he assures me, lightly squeezing my knee.

"I've done it so badly…"

"Why didn't you stay and fix things with her?" he insists.

"Because I knew that sooner or later, the time would come to return, and it has," I explain, though it's a vague excuse that even I don't believe.

"You could have said no and stayed there," he reminds me.

"But it's the best opportunity of my life, Bill; how could I say no?"

"Deep down, you did say no, but to love. You gave up having by your side a woman who understood you and loved you. A person who was willing to be by your side despite the fear your job provides."

A dagger would have hurt less. He's the only one who knows everything about me since I was little. When my parents died in that car accident, me being of legal age, he looked after me and helped me whenever I needed it. That's why he knows that truth would hurt me, though I needed to hear it.

"Gabriela," he whispers, squeezing my knee again, "life is too short to let go of people who love you as much as Emma. Look at me. You know how sorry I am for not having spent more time with my wife before she passed away. And she understood until the end. But when she left, my heart broke. I remembered the thousands of moments I lost being by her side because of my work. And yes, work is important, but love is even more so. You always think there will be time later, but time runs out eventually, and life needs to be lived when it comes."

"I love what I do. I love flying, William, and nothing and no one can change that," I confess.

"Emma didn't change it, quite the opposite; she supported you. She'd have her doubts and fears, of course, she didn't want to lose you. But she supported you and would be there waiting for you after each mission. I'm going to be very honest with you," he adds, getting up and heading to the door. "No professional achievement will compensate if you have no one to share it with. Coming home from a mission and being able to kiss and hug the love of your life is the greatest reward you'll ever have. So, daughter, think about it; we won't be here forever."

A new dagger that sinks even deeper.

***

I lift the weights above my chest to do the last press with which I'll finish today's workout. I've increased the weight by several pounds to try to push myself. I complete the first round with effort. The second is even more costly, fatigue takes its toll. I prepare to do the third, however, after two pushes, I run out of air. I drop the dumbbells to my side. A sharp pain in my chest and lack of air begin to frighten me. I try to sit up, but it's impossible. I let myself fall and end up on the floor, in even more pain.

Not being able to take even a breath of air scares me more and more. Something isn't right. I try to breathe hard, but air doesn't come. The pressure increases; it's a very strange suffocation that spreads throughout my chest. My heart races, I try to stay calm; still, panic overwhelms me. My hands begin to shake, and sweat runs down my temple.

I try to scream, to ask for help, but my throat only produces a kind of high-pitched whistle. I instinctively bring my hand to my chest, pressing as if I could force my lungs to breathe. It's not like drowning. When you drown, at least you have the resistance of water to fight against. This is worse. You fight against nothingness. My body demands oxygen that doesn't reach my lungs, and each attempt to breathe feels like a knife stabbing my side.

"A doctor! We need a doctor!" shout some officers who have just entered the gym.

"I can't die like this," I try to say, though no words come out of my mouth. "It won't be in combat, it won't be shot down by enemy fire. It will be in a damn gym. What a shitty irony of fate."

My entire body shakes with spasm. The pain in my chest becomes unbearable, as if my lungs had filled with broken glass. And then I think of Emma, of her green eyes, of the future we had dreamed together... of all the things I should have told her. Of how much I love her.

New voices, white uniforms. Someone cuts my shirt.

"Pneumothorax. Tension. We need to decompress it right now," someone yells.

They lift me onto a stretcher while shouting for me to stay calm, and the journey to the military hospital is a whirlwind of lights and shadows.

And pain. Extreme pain.

"Periorbital cyanosis, tachycardia. Confirming tension pneumothorax. Preparing decompression," one of the doctors indicates.

"You'll feel a prick," a woman murmurs beside me as she applies alcohol to my skin. "We need to insert a needle to release the pressure that's crushing your lungs."

And then it happens.

A hiss like that of a punctured tire. The sensation that follows is indescribable. Pure bliss. A release so immediate and dramatic that makes you want to cry with emotion. Air begins to enter my collapsed lungs again, at first little by little, but it brings the oxygen my body needs. There's pain with each breath, but it's a pain that brings life, not death, and the feeling of suffocation disappears almost immediately.

"Saturation rising... 82...85."

"We've got you, Night Hawk. The worst is over," one of the doctors mutters.

A few hours later

I suppose pain is a good sign. Proof that I'm still alive, but I hate being in a bed connected to a drainage system.

"How are you feeling, Major Díaz? You gave us quite a scare," greets a tall doctor with gray hair as he approaches the monitor and notes my vital signs.

"I guess I've been much better," I mutter.

"Let me introduce you to Dr. McGrath, our thoracic surgeon. We're going to listen to those lungs, okay? I need you to breathe when we tell you. It will hurt a little," he warns.

"The right lung is expanding again without difficulty," announces the doctor. "Do you remember what happened?"

"I was lifting some dumbbells; suddenly I felt a kind of snap, and then I couldn't breathe," I explain.

"You suffered a tension pneumothorax in both lungs. It's extremely serious. Luckily, we were able to treat it in time. Do you see these small spots?" she asks, pointing to the CT scan images they've taken of me. "They're bullae at the apex of the right lung. So you understand, they're like small bubbles in the lung tissue. Due to exertion, one of them ruptured, releasing air into the pleural space."

"Is that common?" I inquire, trying to understand.

"In people like you, tall, thin, with little body fat, more frequent than it seems."

"Will I need surgery?"

The doctors look at each other, as if drawing straws for who will deliver the news.

"Under normal conditions, it might not be necessary," the woman explains. "However, for a fighter pilot, subjected to tremendous stress, the risk of it happening again is high and something we cannot allow to happen while you're piloting a fighter jet. That would be…" She doesn't need to finish the sentence.

"The left lung is better," the doctor hastens to announce, possibly seeing my angry face.

"How long for recovery?" I growl.

"Six to eight weeks before flying. Maybe more."

"Can you schedule the surgery for this afternoon? I don't want to waste more time than necessary," I protest.

The doctors look at each other again, and the woman raises her eyebrows, shaking her head as if indicating I'm half crazy.

"First we need to stabilize those lungs, Major. But we'll schedule the surgery as soon as possible," she assures me.

As soon as they leave, I close my eyes and start to fall asleep, but the knock of knuckles on the door prevents it.

"Díaz," he greets with a nod.

"Colonel."

"Lately, you've been giving us too many scares," I smile.

"I assure you I don't do it on purpose," I murmur, making him smile too.

"Are you feeling better?"

"A little, though I'm looking at surgery and too much rest ahead."

"You'll get through this on your own two feet, as always," he adds confidently. "But I haven't come just to see how you are. We need to talk."

"Talk?" I question seriously.

"Yes. Your performance here hasn't been as expected," I swallow, confused, since I haven't done anything outside my routine.

"Sir..."

"No, Díaz, I'm going to speak now."

Chapter 21

Emma

The Literary Café is packed to the rafters; the idea of offering a small discount once a month works perfectly. Luckily, I have Lucille's help because it would be impossible to manage alone. In recent weeks, though she refused at first, I ended up hiring her. She enjoys the work, and for me, an extra pair of hands has been a tremendous help, not just for day-to-day operations but to take days off, something that had barely happened since the day I opened.

With my friend by my side, everything has become much easier; I could even say that customers do their part. A few curious people asked about Gabriela, but it's been more than a month since that happened. I still think about her daily, but I know she's fulfilling her dream, that she'll be happy, and that helps me.

A little, but it helps.

Near the end of the morning shift, an unexpected visitor appears in the café.

"Oh my God," Lucille whispers when she sees him. I hadn't noticed him yet.

"Daniel…" I sigh as he approaches. "What are you doing here?"

"I want to know why you haven't answered my calls these past few weeks."

"Do you really want me to explain?" I question with a half-smile. "I'm done with you, Daniel. I can't be clearer than that. I just want you to disappear from my life once and for all," Lucille smiles beside me. "What I don't understand is why you keep insisting on calling me."

"I need your help."

"My help?" I repeat, confused.

"They caught me with a few too many drinks after having an accident while driving. Well, the thing is, my income has dropped since I can't drive, and I need to pay a lawyer. I need you to lend me some money."

"What do you think this is? A bank?" Lucille blurts out, making me laugh. He tries to say something, but I don't allow it.

"Don't even think about saying a word, Daniel. She's right," I add, crossing my arms over my chest. "First of all, deal with it; next time, don't drink before getting behind the wheel. And second, I wouldn't have helped you anyway."

"That woman has brainwashed you; you're not like this. You should…"

"I don't owe anything, Daniel, that woman didn't brainwash me."

"She ate other things, to tell the truth," my friend says, making me blush and laugh, causing him to become even more furious.

"Look, you'd better leave and not show up here again. Forget me forever. I'm not going to give you anything or help you. You're not part of my life, and you never will be again," I warn him, pointing toward the door with my index finger.

"Someday you'll regret this," he says, trying to intimidate me.

"I don't think so," I respond, confident in myself and maintaining my smile, prompting his departure and, finally, or so I hope, ensuring he won't return here.

Lucille raises her arm to high-five me playfully as he exits through the door.

"That's my girl!" she exclaims, making me laugh.

Our laughter fills the place with good vibes, at last. Our smiles widen when we see Rick appear. Lately, he comes often to buy breakfast for Lucille. Since the little one was born, these small treats help her start the morning on the right foot. In fact, I'm surprised to see him for the second time today:

"More sweets?" I question, puzzled.

"More like a favor," he says, leaning on the counter. "Could you go for a couple of hours to keep Melissa company? You know she needs rest," I nod. "They called me to resolve something urgent at the base, and I couldn't say no."

"Go, I'll stay here," Lucille indicates before I can answer.

"Sure, let me change, and I'll be right there."

"Thank you so much," he whispers, putting his hands together in a gesture of gratitude. "Oh, Emma, don't make lunch plans, I'll bring something over later."

Once at Melissa and Ghost's house, the little one sleeps like an angel, giving us both a chance to catch up. I've been so busy that I haven't been able to visit as much as I'd like.

"You look much better."

"I am, although the C-section scar is quite bothersome."

"That's normal, Mel, after all, it's surgery. But little by little, you'll improve and can return to normal. The important thing is that both you and the baby are well. Is she giving you a hard time? I don't think I heard her cry once in the first few days."

"It depends on the day," she says with a smile, as she leans over to caress the baby's cheek with the back of her hand. "She only cries when she wants to eat, at least for now. Rick does me the favor and gets up when she needs it in the middle of the night, he's such a great dad."

"Yes, he really is," I nod.

During all the time we're there, until the little one cries for her next feeding, we spend it talking about our daily lives; I update her on the café, and she tells me how she feels since becoming a mother. When it's time, she allows me to give the bottle, which I appreciate. Those little brown eyes, similar to her father's, stare at me intently. I don't look up until I hear the door and see Rick appear.

"Bottle feeding suits you," he jokes with a smile, approaching to caress the little one's forehead.

"You have a beautiful daughter," I say, looking back at her.

"Weren't you going to buy lunch?" Melissa asks, looking at him while raising her eyebrows.

"Yes, that's right."

"And where is it?" she protests.

"I have it."

Her voice.

I never thought I'd hear it again in my life.

I lift my gaze from the baby almost fearfully and confirm I'm not dreaming. She's here, Gabriela is here, and she looks at me with a smile that stirs my entire stomach, just like the first time she did it.

Chapter 22

Gabriela

Emma and Melissa's eyes lock onto me the moment they hear me speak. Neither of them knew anything, just as I'd asked Ghost. He quickly helps Mel to her feet, eager to embrace me.

"I can't believe it! What are you doing here?" she asks happily, breaking the hug only to embrace me again, as if she doesn't believe I'm really standing in front of her.

"It was time to visit my beautiful goddaughter, wasn't it?" I respond, pleased. It's one of the reasons I'm here, though not the most important one.

They both step aside, allowing me to approach the baby and Emma, who remains with her in her arms, completely stunned and frozen in place.

"Hi…" I sigh. "I see the little one, and you are getting along well."

She inhales in stages, and I notice how her eyes fill with tears in an instant. I glance at my friend, and with a simple look, he understands. He takes the baby and gestures to Melissa for them to leave us alone.

"What are you doing here?" she questions, crying, as soon as they leave. "I thought we wouldn't see each other again… At least, that I wouldn't."

"I thought the same, but I've realized the terrible mistake I made. A few weeks ago, I suffered a pneumothorax in both lungs while training," I tell her, kneeling in front of her and placing my hands on her legs. "I couldn't breathe and even began to think I wouldn't make it."

"What? But… but are you okay?" she asks, sitting up straighter and coming closer, her tone and gaze full of concern.

"Yes, I had surgery, and I'm practically recovered, though they still won't let me fly," I add, reassuring her. "But what I'm getting at is that during that moment when I thought I would die, just like during the accident, there was only one thing that crossed my mind," she looks at me questioningly. "You. I made a tremendous mistake pushing you away—the worst mistake of my life. Every day since then, I've missed you. Not a single day has passed since I left that I haven't fallen asleep crying, regretting what I did."

"Gabriela…"

"Let me finish, please," I ask, feeling the moisture from my eyes begin to run down my cheeks. "Emma, I didn't act well. I'm so sorry for how I treated you. I'm deeply sorry for leaving this way. I regret it every day and will for the rest of my life. That's why I've come back. I want you to give me another chance for us to start over. All I want is to be with you."

"But what about your job? Your position in the United States? I don't want you to give it up for me, Gabriela. I…"

"I'm coming back to Zelenova, Emma, and this time for good."

"What? But…" I place my fingers on her lips, preventing her from speaking so she'll listen to me.

"While in recovery, my Colonel came to visit me…"

"Sir…"

"No, Díaz, I'm going to speak now," I nodded, having felt those words as an order. "I know you well, Díaz. You always adapt very well to any of your bases and team. However, since you returned

from Atrivia, you haven't been the same. That place has changed you."

"Too many things happened in too little time. And perhaps I left behind what I love most and what made me happiest."

"A tremendous error, if I may add. I made the same mistake many years ago, and that's why I'm here today," I was surprised by his words. "I've given a lot of thought to what I'm going to tell you, Díaz, and, although I'm going to lose the best pilot in the entire United States, I have something to offer you."

"What do you want to offer me, sir?" I ask, confused.

"Your position became vacant in Atrivia. Ghost is there, your team is there..."

"Emma is also there," I whispered, looking at him.

"I want you to return and resume your position, indefinitely."

"I didn't even think about it. In fact, I wanted them to transfer me immediately so I could finish my recovery here, but they wouldn't allow it," Emma smiles; I'm stubborn even while convalescing.

"So... does this mean you're staying here forever?"

194

"Yes. My work, my people, you… Everything I want is here," she smiles before I can wipe away her tears. "Can you forgive me?" I ask, pressing my forehead to hers, releasing all the air and nerves I have inside.

"I forgave you the same night you left, Gabriela," I open my eyes, incredulous at hearing her words. "I knew your fears, I had them too. I let you go because I knew your work made you happy. They weren't easy days, we didn't handle it well."

"Me even less than you," I admit.

"But you're here, betting on us again. And for me, that's a big step," she assures me, taking my hands in hers.

"Does that mean you'll give me a chance?"

"Yes, Gabriela," as soon as I hear her, I dive for her lips, making her smile. "Though I won't make it too easy for you…" she jokes, pulling me to sit on her lap and embrace her.

"I love you, Emma Carter, since the first time I saw you at the Literary Café," I sigh against her lips.

"I love you too, Gabriela, I haven't stopped for a single moment."

And there, in her arms, I understand that I'm finally where I want to be. Home, in the place where I'm truly happy and where we're going to create our own story.